Carbine

D1565192

Carbine

Stories

Greg Mulcahy

University of Massachusetts Press
Amherst & Boston

LC 2010007643
ISBN 978-1-55849-818-1

Designed by Sally Nichols
Set in Myriad Pro and Adobe Jenson Pro
Printed and bound by Lightning Source, Inc.

Library of Congress Cataloging-in-Publication Data

Mulcahy, Greg.
Carbine : stories / Greg Mulcahy.
p. cm.
ISBN 978-1-55849-818-1 (pbk. : alk. paper)
I. Title.
PS3563.U389C33 2010
813'.54—dc22
2010007643

British Library Cataloguing in Publication data are available.

For my love, Abigail

Many of the stories in this collection appeared, in identical or slightly different form, in *Gettysburg Review, Mississippi Mud, Communitas, Phantasmagoria, Noon, Strawberry Press, elimae, Snow Monkey, Juked, Word Riot, 5-trope, Alice Blue, Sidebrow, Anemone Sidecar,* and *New York Tyrant.* The author thanks the editors of these journals.

Contents

Carbine

Hat

There was a theoretical problem, not that he thought it would go beyond theory, not in his case, in others' cases, sure, for them the theoretical was real, but what was so odd about that, for after all, if one thought about it, was not every theoretical problem based in the real, or, to take it further, to get to what he was implying, to get to what he really thought but would not say aloud, wasn't every theoretical problem a real problem for someone but usually not, and he hoped never, for him? He was in the Catholic cemetery on business of his own when he started thinking about it: Suppose a man with a gun comes to the front door of the house and says he wants it all. There were no victims buried there he knew of to get him thinking about it; no, that was not it at all. In fact, the problem, the question as he framed it, was not the problem, not the original problem stated earlier in the week at work; at work the problem which was introduced by the Head of Security, no he had that wrong, it was the Chief of Security—he had not known there was one—naturally he had never thought about it, but he wasn't an idiot; if he had thought about it, he would certainly have realized that there was someone in charge of security, that security, as the Chief had said, did not just happen, but that was not the question, nor were his speculations about the Chief and the man with the gun at his door; the question was what would you do if a disgruntled former employee with a gun showed up in your department. The Chief did not have to state the rest, to explain the disgruntled former employee would be there for revenge, would be, in fact, shooting everyone in sight. And what would he do? He would do anything necessary to save his life, he thought. He would, he thought, dive under his desk and hide there. He thought he would jump through the window. He would run to the store room and barricade himself inside, he thought, until help arrived. He thought he would plead, he would whine, he would beg for his life.

But not at home. At home he would get his gun and take care of the problem. Oh, he had a gun. Just like everybody else. He was not allowed to bring it to work. There was a strict policy. No one was allowed to possess weapons on company property, although from what the Chief said, it seemed like maybe the company should reconsider. But at home, at home he had his gun and nobody was going to barge in and trouble him, and nobody was going to disarm him, he did not want to hear any more about that, they could pass all the fucking laws they wanted to, he was hanging onto his gun.

Given the setting, of course, he thought, he was bound to think, that when the time came he hoped he would die in a bloody fight.

All the flat stones. Now one had to have one; no other kind was allowed.

The sun out and the afternoon on, going on now with the warmth coming up, and some birds flying above the lake on the other side of the hill he was climbing, the hill that at its peak overlooked the lake, the stone-studded hill with the familiar names on the stones, the family names common to his neighborhood, to his part of the city. Thinking for a second on the names of those lost in that cold hill, he considered what he should give up: liquor, cigarettes, red meat. And thought then who was he, Polydeuces, to be giving things up? And the sun high, he found himself squinting, the light harsh as though he had a hangover, and he felt thick and stupid. This attitude, this aggravation, this fuck-with-me-and-I'll-shoot-you mentality, not him at all, although familiar to him, the type of thinking he might engage in if he had a hangover although clearly he did not, had not had a hangover in years. When he had had them, he noticed that hungover he could often see the past. Not the literal past, but it had seemed that the past was upon him in a way that he would, for example, go into a mall or a grocery store and see a woman who looked exactly like a woman he had known when he was twenty, exactly as the woman had looked, or as he remembered her as having looked, twenty years before: This could not be the same woman, for the woman, like anyone, would not look as she had looked twenty years in the past, and it was never any woman he had known well, just some woman he knew casually or was in a class with or had found attractive. And why not, why wouldn't he see someone as in the past, for didn't everyone see himself as he was or thought he was twenty years ago? But he was not really seeing the person, not the person he was thinking of, he was seeing someone who reminded him of the person he was thinking of, not really seeing either person with any clarity. And women, what would he say to a woman he had known if he were to see one now? He would have to think of what to say, think hard until something occurred to him, and what ever had occurred to him through thought that was worth mentioning to anyone?

He was at the top of the hill and thought was the last thing he wanted, to think here, on this afternoon, about anything. No. The sun glittered on the lake and the birds flew and called and the trees, the pines at the base of the hill, tall and green surrounding the lake. The water, the trees, the birds, they were, after all, real?

2.

Wearing many hats. That's what got him off track. Ms. Mells had said the thing about the hats and he had thought, or remembered, an extraordinary photograph he had seen of a nude woman wearing only a sailor's hat. The woman was extraordinary, not the photo, a black and white, he supposed the photo, on second thought, was extraordinary too. But that woman. And the hat, of course, the function of the hat was to tell, well to imply, to imply a kind of story.

There had been a conflict and he had to go to class, conflict resolution class or better communication class or new management style leadership class, whatever they called it, but the conflict was not so much his fault as it was inevitable as they should have known when they teamed him with Swanson, Swanson who had been drinking his lunch since he had been passed over two years before for a promotion he felt he had earned, Swanson who would not do anything but complain, obstruct, complain and obstruct any meaningful progress he tried to make as he lugged Swanson, his ball and chain, through the days and weeks toward the deadline they obviously could not make, for the job was a three-man job at least, but with the new lean management two might have been able to do it, two who worked hard, kicked ass, but not he and most certainly not he and Swanson, Swanson who was due in the future, the near future, for a punishment, a big punishment, but who was, for now, his punishment, for Swanson's punishment would wait, would keep until he was well and thoroughly punished, his punishment being the priority among the two.

Now in the class on a Saturday, after all, this was auxiliary duty, not on company time, on this Saturday with the winter air drier than the air in the Sahara, that was a fact, that was how dry the air was in the conference room, the conference room that looked like, was modeled on, a hotel ball room with Ms. Mells, the facilitator, whose bland and stylized appearance recalled a former Miss Minnesota gone over to some helping profession, talking.

This was a famous photograph, it turned out, by a photographer of great renown, but the woman, the model, well, he did not know anything about that. Her. About her.

Ms. Mells said a series of things which were not true.

A fish, he thought the saying went, rots from the head down. And what, he wondered, about a man? He had always thought a man would be more generalized, starting everywhere at once, at the same time, but now he was equally certain this could not be correct. And he, he had apparently expected that they would thank him for standing up in a more or less public meeting and saying their numbers were all wrong, that the spreadsheets, their goddamned spreadsheets, were for all intents and purposes meaningless. If only he would accept and behave as though he fully felt what he knew, had known for years, that they were all liars, that everyone lied, that every utterance, every word, was a lie and could not be anything other than a lie.

Ms. Mells with her big manila tablet on a stand that looked like an artist's easel and her set of colorful magic markers. Ms. Mells drew a big red package labeled GOAL with a big blue bow labeled PLANNING.

This, he thought, is something to see.

And Swanson, if there were any justice in this false world, Swanson would be in the ground, or better, more just, he would put Swanson in the ground. All Swanson had done for three months—the duration of the project—was read some sociological tome called *Belief and the Model Prisoner* and swear at him in Spanish. Swear words were about the only Spanish words he knew, and he was not sure how he had learned them, but he himself swore in Spanish quite frequently. He was not even sure why he did this. Maybe it seemed more effective, as if the Spanish were more powerful than the English.

And what was it with the sailor's hat? And this photograph had nothing, nothing whatsoever to do with the model. Sure she had a life, went home to her kids, the picture with its hat, its implied story, nothing like her. That idea that the camera stole your soul had it backwards. If the sailor, a sailor, if there had been a sailor and if the sailor had taken the picture, it would have turned out badly. Rotten composition, poor lighting, no focus. Her eyes shut. It would have turned out like a black and white version of the pictures of their girlfriends men sent to skin mags.

Anyway, what did it matter? If he saw that picture again now, he probably would not recognize it given the thorough distortion—the falsity—of memory. A picture—when the question was who would attrite him. When? Maybe he'd be out before the collapse.

Yeah, maybe he'd win the lottery.

Ms. Mells was handing out legal pads and sharp, shiny, new pencils. The falsehoods were flying thicker and faster now. It was a story telling exercise, she said, that would allow them to assess and reveal their true personalities.

How could he begin? Where? He hated stories. To start in about Molly and his home life—why say anything? What was this compulsion to extract confessions and to confess nowadays?

Ms. Mells said to write down the story, but it had to be true, absolutely true.

How had they dropped him here, him and not Swanson? How, really, had anything happened to him? Wasn't he, after all, only a talking ape?

All he wanted was to think about the picture, and now as he looked at the yellow, lined paper, he didn't know anything to say. Knowledge was useless, irrelevant here; why not abandon personal history? Personality? After all what was it but a kind of knowledge, false as any other?

And the hat. What about the hat?

At that moment, he made his vow.

3.

Molly talked about the natural state it seemed or the state of nature. The natural order, that was what she was speaking of. And to what end he could not have said. She got these ideas and was all on about them until they faded away or disappeared. She had wanted, for example, a year ago to move away from the city and buy a small property in the country where they would make their living organically growing herbs. He did not know what herbs were worth, but it seemed quite clear to him that, organic or not, herbs were not worth much.

What he wanted was some lunch. What the fuck was natural law?

An herb farm. An herb farm was called a garden, wasn't it? It was not really a farm; it was maybe an acre.

She knew he would like to retire, but he had nothing put by.

Molly said something about the look on his face.

She was on him all the time with some kind of accusation when he wanted what—what had he ever wanted—but some lunch. There was a place he knew, a Greek place where he could get the best gyros in town and fries, and that place was not too far away. He told her he'd buy her lunch if she wanted to come along.

He was engaged in some questionable practices for his own benefit.

Those were her words, not his. That's what she said.

And besides, who wasn't?

After all, hadn't he in the last week heard an anthropologist on TV who said that in the future we'll know much more about the past? If the anthropologists were saying that, why should he bother to defend himself? What kind of people grew herbs for that matter? What did Molly want, worse, what did she imagine, that he'd grow a long, gray beard and wear bib overalls while she pranced around barefoot in a flower-printed sundress on the brilliant summer afternoons? Or perhaps from herbs they could branch out, start bottling honey and making furniture out of willow twigs. No one would want to live like that, yet she imagined it a paradise, a new world of opportunity and pleasure with some older world of sun and moon and cyclical seasons embedded within it.

Natural order. Look at this neighborhood. The houses and the picture windows and the cars in the drives. All silent now, on this Monday at 1:00 p.m. This was not the language he and Molly had shared. That language was long gone, and now there was nothing, not a thing in this world, to say. The cars, the houses, the picture windows realized it, it had taken him some time longer, as they waited, as he waited now, grinning uncomfortably, for her to realize the obvious.

Maybe if she did what he did, if she saw what he saw. Last week in the parking lot at work, just as he was about to step over the curb onto the walkway, he noticed something on the ground, some splintered gray plastic on the gray sand-and-cigarette-butt-littered pavement. It took him a second to recognize it for what it was—a crushed computer disk—and he thought this is something new, something that did not exist when he was a kid, and here it was, the advent of techno-trash.

And in her state of nature what would they be relegated to? To huddle there at night beside the fire after a backbreaking day in the unending series of the same that was their life?

He was still hungry. He was not going to stop being hungry until he got something.

All fine and good to buy the magazines about simple living and the rest of it, but he knew what she was really talking about was a new life. All right, who could stop himself from imagining that?

The other day at Burger King he saw this guy, a guy in a blue pinstriped suit. The suit was cheap, not what it was supposed to be, but an indication of what it wanted to be, and the guy had a Bible. The guy was eating his Whopper while he read the Bible in that noisy, crowded fast-food store. He could tell her about the new life, the new life they could actually get, and that was, he feared, coming bidden or unbidden, with or without Bibles and Burger King.

Doll

There was smoke and the fucking thing went off and he had to disconnect it and he broke it. Poor fucking design, that's what kept them selling. The little plastic hooks the housing hung from got soft and failed as anyone could see they would. A fifteen-cent latch a far superior mechanism but then they would not break after four openings and few would be sold.

He needed a working one. He needed to know a working one was downstairs though he reminded himself there was a time when such alarms did not exist. When he was a kid no one had one because they did not exist. And remember this—when he was a kid, everyone smoked all the time.

Things burned of course.

That, and people died. Not everybody. Not every day. Now and then. As now. He wasn't sure if more died then or now. It was one of those things—he had not been paying attention.

If his house went up in the night, you understand, he did not want to burn or choke and die. If it were working, he might have a chance. Without it, he suspected he would have no chance whatsoever.

He feared sometimes he'd never wake up.

Or he'd wake up and suffer horribly in horror until his agonizing end.

It had happened to others and he knew he was no better than them.

And no stronger. If he were strong enough, that might help, but he was not.

One was overcome, you know.

That was how it happened.

He remembered the crazy bastard he'd found on a bus stop bench when he was sixteen, seventeen years old. The crazy bastard called out to him, begged him to help. Help? This guy was fifty, sixty years old. The crazy bastard wanted help getting to his house, a rickety depression brick model maybe two hundred feet from the bench. The crazy bastard was drunk or crazy or both but he half-carried the bastard to the house and got the bastard stretched out on the couch and in the course of it noticed how emaciated and sallow—jaundiced—the bastard was and he knew the bastard would be dead soon.

A dying old bastard.

The house crammed with stacked newspaper and shitty church sale furniture.

The old bastard asked him to go to the gas station and buy some cigarettes—Chesterfields or some fucking brand nearly extinct even then. He did it and when he got back, the crazy bastard told him a confused tale about some woman the bastard had done everything for who had inevitably taken everything and left now that the bastard was sick and helpless.

Even at fifteen or sixteen, he knew the bastard's self-pity was infinite. The bastard talked while he studied the faded paint visible between the stacks of newspaper. Then he left.

The bastard asked him to stay. He was as happy leaving that house as he was leaving any house.

If he needed help, whom would he beg?

If he'd learned anything about begging, it was to leave the self-pity out of it.

And the bums.

He'd heard some guys burned one down at the river. Poured gas over him and lit him up. Back in the time of the crazy bastard. All the bum stories then, the quasi-mythical yet frequently seen bums of that time as disposable as children in fairy tales.

Worked then as a dishwasher in a hospital in a bad area. A building abandoned maybe nearby or maybe still renting in its near total decay.

Bums stayed there.

And it burned. Somebody said the bums lit it on fire when they were drunk. On purpose or by accident was unclear. Two killed too drunk to notice or too drunk to leave. They found one, it was said, in a front room dead of smoke inhalation.

But the other.

The other, the story went, realized there was a fire so he filled the bathtub and got in, not realizing the water would heat. And it did. To a boil.

Word was when they found him he had split like an overcooked hot dog.

He did not know if that could happen. And why bums anyway? And all this past? Hadn't he slipped two of them down on the flats when he was eleven, two he feared wanted to fuck him?

When he was seventeen, they were trying to force his father out at work by humiliating his father.

His father walked in the door one night and said, They burned me down, burned me down like a paper doll.

Remember that Old Hot Dog?

Not long after, he left the house and never saw his father again.

He wheezed and drank and drank and wheezed and glanced at his swollen, sallow face in the mirror.

Jaune

Recalled to their purpose, he put his hand decisively on her breast.

This was long ago. She wore those plastic shoes that were supposed to protect the feet from hazards on the beach.

Or was this long ago and she wore a thin gold chain?

It was said that at one time in China, yellow was the color associated with the emperor and only members of the imperial family were permitted to wear it.

Maybe this was a long time ago and she was wearing a crisp, lemon-colored dress.

Baby, he said, I need you.

Baby, he said, I feel like I'm about to explode.

He thought he had made comments along those lines, but he understood he was, in all of this, more or less a figure of allegory.

While all of this was going on, meanwhile, somebody somewhere was reinventing the notion of music. Then, he was doing the best he could under what seemed like impossible circumstances. Now, he had a catalog of sexual practice, but no one wanted to hear about that anymore. He knew he had his devils.

Everyone had his own devils.

His devil, he was certain, was a dangerous one and likely to kill him. His secret heart hoped he would find her whose love would save him, rescue him, arm him against himself. Outside his secret heart, he thought all the years of his experience indicated that this was unlikely.

Did he think himself jaundiced?

Maybe he was sallow. Maybe he could not help being sallow.

Perhaps every story begins in topography and we simply do not know it. Whatever the case, he did not want to think about it.

Sometimes he thought he should raise her and they should sail to the Green Isle of Sentiment and lead charmed lives there.

He knew this notion and knew that shortly it would fade like invisible ink fades into invisibility. He recognized that trick from when he was a boy. When he was a boy, every boy knew this trick. It had been, then, a part of being a boy.

Yet as he held her in the close embrace and ran his hand over her smooth, perfectly-formed breast it seemed the only topography was the physical, the delight of her body the whole story, the entire pursuit of his life.

She was laughing.

He was smiling, he guessed.

You'll be to blame, she laughed. If you go any further, you'll have only yourself to blame.

He laughed at that. What blame could accrue but the blame he wanted right then more than anything in the world?

She was, after all, unbuttoning his shirt.

Now later, many years after this, he felt he needed a lot of pockets to carry his things—the notebook he needed to mitigate his failing memory; the banana and apple he had to eat every day, for everyone was for fruit now, right; his sunglasses; his reading glasses; his pen and pencil set.

His colleague had a green, multipocketed, paramilitary vest that he admired, but his colleague camped and fished all the time—an outdoorsman.

He told the woman about this vest.

—A vest, she said, is not a vestment.

He understood. It was similar to the time he wanted the special car. He'd wanted to buy the safest car in the world so they'd be fully protected.

She had told him as well that he was going deaf although he was quite certain that he was not deaf and was not going deaf. If he were—after she'd said that he became a little self conscious about it—he'd show them when his hearing was gone. He'd demand full accommodation, everything he was entitled to by law.

Then, all those years ago, though, she unbuttoned his shirt. She loved him, maybe. Certainly she was interested in him. He was not sure of anything, but he, simultaneously, seemed to think that anything was possible. He seemed impervious to learning what could not be done then, in that moment.

There were cars and clothes and music—all the backdrop of the culture and his touchstone in it, but then they seemed unreal—absent—outside of that moment.

He told her to cup it in her hand.

It was the invention of the sentence.

Later he would think about this.

He always wanted to be the Strong Man. Back then and after right into the now as well. He was lazy though. It was hard—the weights, the road work, the discipline. It took a lot of time and effort to be the strength made flesh.

He told her they had to put a simple gloss over everything. He used the phrase *needs must*. That was not characteristic of him.

He was holding his glass; thick but not too heavy, it fit neatly in his hand. He took a drink. His glass, V-shaped, recalled to him other deltas where he had lain and rested.

Again he thought of strength and weakness—his many failings.

He took another drink.

What curse was laid upon him?

Who had laid this curse upon him?

Her breath smelled like meat tenderizer.

Her breath smelled like metal.

Her breath smelled like alcohol.

Her breath had smelled like paradise.

Had he really sold himself, his future, his happiness, many times since then?

This really happened.

First his lip went numb. Not the entire lip, but the area of his upper lip to the left of his nose went numb. An area maybe an inch long, numb for brief periods. It was an occasional thing, a thing he noticed every once in awhile.

Then it became more frequent.

He thought he had somehow damaged the nerve and tried to recall an occasion when he had injured his face. Of course he had been struck in the face a few times, but never, in his recollection, to any great consequence. The odd ball had hit him too, but nothing serious.

Soon the numbness was constant.

Then it spread to almost the entire lip.

His lip twisted. He looked like he was snarling. Or sneering. He was not sure what to do. Clearly he had to get to a doctor, but the evolution of his condition had been so gradual that he could not imagine the cause was anything drastic.

He wanted to tell her about it but he was not sure if she would laugh at him.

He had asked her lately if he could videotape her naked; this had nothing to do with the state of his lip. As far as he could recall, his request may have predated any problem with his lip. He had wanted her to stand there naked and laughing while he videotaped her but he did not want to bring his malady into that proposal. He knew that now that he was physically hampered his complaint would have to come into it, from her point of view, if only subliminally.

It was then he wanted to quit the city.

This lip thing was obviously a harbinger of something debilitating and possibly of something lethal and it seemed the culmination of all his myriad discontents.

But he really wanted to videotape her. If only she'd answer him, yet it was her strategy to remain noncommittal.

He had not had one in years, but suddenly he wanted a boiled egg. And why? It wasn't going to help his lip any although perhaps he had some dim association from childhood of the egg as a healing food.

She would have to laugh seriously into the camera if she were to laugh into it at all.

The whole point was to present the complicated architecture of everything in miniature.

Yes, he wanted to quit the city.

Lately he had been spending time near the pond on the campus, in the woods there, until it seemed too many had remarked on it.

Now he was the man with the twisted lip.

He had it all planned. He could just say—Listen, Baby, won't you be my everything? He'd said this years before.

She served him some kind of yellow fish for supper. It was in a thick yellow sauce—almost a paste. The paste was yellow, but the fish was some kind of yellow fish too—that was in the fish's name. She told him, but now it had slipped his mind.

He had forgotten.

What yellow fish was that?

Some of the paste had got stuck under his fingernail. He scrubbed his hands repeatedly, but it was still there three days later. The yellow fish fingernails.

He thought she thought it was too late for cameras.

Would she have done it all those years ago?

She had pulled off her top then, after he had unbuttoned his shirt. And then, and then, she shook her head to straighten her hair. She did this automatically, unconsciously, but he remembered it. The image.

He walked then. He had no car, and he enjoyed walking. The city then hadn't lost all its big trees to blight, and for a city, it was a green place. In the residential areas, at least.

Was it the fall then? The sky always gray in his memory as the sky now was always gray in the fall. He walked under the gray that was over the green. He was beneath the green that was covered by the gray. But in autumn, in say, Indian summer, hadn't there been sun? Bright sun through the colored leaves? He wanted to walk in that lemon yellow light.

What if it were as though he were a prisoner imprisoned in his own life? When he was a child, they had taken great pains to teach him to suffer. Not that he was in any way abused, or even ill-treated, but it was always the mortification of this and the denial of that.

Well, he had hated them for it and for the dull, shriveled life it would lead him.

How could he have understood that the suffering he was compelled to execute was the practice of suffering, the practice to prepare himself for the greater suffering that was to come?

He saw himself unaided by these exercises.

At work, on his floor, in the stairwell, a big, yellow 3 was painted on the concrete wall.

And did he, and, if not, why didn't he, buy her a silken robe to see her in it in the sunny rooms in the mornings?

This was all a long time ago and maybe he remembered it wrong. Even the past could be a mistake. Even the past was disappearing now.

He thought he had had—he thought he was opening—back then—the secret book of all. He did not, if he had ever had it, have it now. And he could not explain how he had lost it. What was he supposed to do, remember and recount the flat story of love?

It wasn't him coupled the Latin with the Gaelic.

Or put it another way—back then, all those years ago, he had never been promised that she would be who he wanted her to be.

That anyone would be.

As if those were the magic words.

On the other hand, he thought it was all him.

He watched the *nature* program on TV. Having watched this spectacle of natural abundance, he knew God's mind was strange to him, and he was tempted to seek *mercy* in it.

This *nature* program filled him with grief.

He thought it was all him and if there was no *mercy* in the mind of God, he should perhaps seek to erase every individuating characteristic of himself.

They could bury him with anonymous office furniture.

The Holy Text, as he recalled, was not much for comedy.

It was all him—these conscious constructs, these illusions—were his own, and as such, his fault. His faults. His sin against himself with no respite.

The tiresome snare of thought.

And against it?

A thing. Like a lemon. Beauty of the fruit. Tart. The skin. Flavor. Raw. Everything it added. Everything it was.

Gallery

She had not done anything.

He had expected her to. To do something. Every indication was she was going to do something.

But there she was. Absent. Silent. Invisible in her inactivity.

It was as though she has ceased to be.

He thought he could recreate her.

But he'd done that already. The idea made him weary. Would he have to do it again?

He knew he could not stop himself. Yet he blamed her. There was only she to blame. She was the one who, for all her promise, had not, apparently, bothered to do a goddamned thing.

It was her callousness. Her self-centered refusal. That's what got to him. She could go along as though she did not exist, without musing, without thinking, without dreaming he was out there.

She could act as though she cared nothing about it.

Silence her sword and shield.

As though she were dead. The ultimate defense. That ultimate defense.

It wasn't THE BOOK OF THE DEAD again, was it? No apparent end to that burden where she was concerned.

He thought he could get away from that. Cease to revisit her there.

This time he thought it could be different.

He'd thought that before.

This time, he said to himself, he'd make her do things.

She wasn't going to create him.

Or had she?

She certainly wasn't actively creating him now with this posture—this do-nothing stance of hers.

You know he could make her the saddest woman in the world. Or the unhappiest. If there were a difference.

See how she'd like that this time.

Perhaps this was not the right approach. Perhaps his bitter hatred of everything drove him to this.

Did he hate everything?

Bitterly?

Maybe at times, but who was consistent? Who had constant emotions?

It could not exist, could it, the constancy of the emotion.

Because.

Because the fixed emotion is no longer an emotion.

It becomes something else.

A compulsion. Maybe.

He had no compulsions in the clinical—the pathological—sense. His compulsions, and he applied the term loosely to himself, were like duties. Things he had to do. Responsibilities.

His responsibility to himself.

She—well, where was she? It was not as though she would or could release him. She did not have the power to release him. She was gone.

She was gone to him.

It was impossible.

All his responsibilities were. Or seemed to be. Yet he was condemned to endure them. To dutifully prosecute them.

Oh, he'd done what he'd had to do.

He made things. That's right; he used to make things.

So did everybody.

What had happened with that anyway?

Make this thing with her in it. Make her into some thing. All because she would not do anything. All this personal nonsense.

What had happened to his hard edge? His refusal to endow anything with meaning? His profound knowledge of the temporal?

Where had all that got to?

Instead, everything was imperfect. And all the imperfections demanded recognition. Acknowledgement. Acceptance.

Really it was giving up all the perfections, wasn't it? The perfection of life, the perfection of art, the perfection of love. None of that. The perfection of nothing.

He'd have to go into his own life.

That life that had become unintended.

That bundle of dulling responsibilities, answered calls.

He had none of all that was promised. He wanted all that was promised. Of course, it had not been promised to him. But knowing that, being fully aware of that, he believed, he held the insistent and unshakable belief that it had been promised to him.

She knew he felt that way.

And what was she doing about it?

Well, she was not riding to his rescue, was she? She was not actively seeking his release, was she? She was not out there doing everything that possibly could be done on his behalf, was she?

It certainly did not seem that way.

Or, there was absolutely no evidence of that.

Or, all indications were negative.

Nothing was going to change any of that.

He knew he should do something, but he also knew there was nothing he could do. He was unable to act effectively to help himself.

He'd go to work.

After all, hadn't he better get to work? Shouldn't he get on with it? Wasn't that what it was *all about?*

There was no use waiting.

No use in being paralyzed into inactivity.

That had happened. Earlier. When he sometimes could not do anything.

His weakness. His laziness. His immense capacity for self-pity was not lost on him.

She'd be of no help. She'd all but told him that.

She'd said he had abandoned her.

That was true, he supposed, as far as it went.

Well, he was not abandoning her now. Was he?

Now he'd make her whatever he wanted. Maybe he wanted her to be the Toy Lady. Had she ever thought of that? Maybe she'd want to be the

Toy Lady. Why would she not or could she not consent to being the Toy Lady?

And if she would not be the Toy Lady, why could he not find another who might be willing to be the Toy Lady?

Many people would consider being the Toy Lady good.

It would be like a role in a movie from a country where food or sex or life was considered good.

Nothing was considered good where he was from.

Don't think that did not shape him somewhat.

When he was younger.

She had claimed, long ago, long ago, before or after all that abandonment talk, she needed some peace. As though he were—what—constant conflict?

Sometimes he thought, given her unwillingness to do anything, that she did not deserve it. She did not deserve one minute, not one second, of the distillation of life he gave her.

The Fantastic Memory of _____.

The Unending Hunger for _____.

And while she was out there doing nothing, did she pity him?

Was he pitiful?

He did not believe she had a right to make any determination at all in that area. It was none of her business, really. Had absolutely nothing to do with her.

Her judgments. If her judgments were so inspired, he wanted to know of any one of her, no doubt, many, many judgments which had proven to be correct. True.

He had not seen any of them up on billboards nor heard them broadcast through the ubiquitous electronic media.

No one was playing that tune. Or even whistling it.

Maybe he'd make her the Whiskey Gal. See how she put up with that.

Who wouldn't want to be the Whiskey Gal, after all?

There was a time, when, to hear her tell it, at that time, she'd do anything. I'll do anything; she told him. That is what she'd said. Exactly that.

She wasn't doing anything now, though.

She had not, as far as he could tell, in his regard, done anything in years.

So what was all this anything worth?

If she would talk—if she would do something—then he would know.

What did she have against a little this and that? What was so wrong with some give and take?

The Toy Lady didn't have any problem with it. The Whiskey Gal, properly lubricated, was all for it.

Of course, they weren't real. He knew that. He was absolutely clear on that.

He had surveyed and he continued to carefully survey what was real. And he had come to some conclusions. He had concluded that the world was different now. It had become another world. Here he was in another world. And he had nothing to say.

Not a word.

Not in this world. He was a mute here.

He knew how limited his options were. He realized he had always known, but earlier, he did not know he'd known nor had he fully understood how narrowly his options were limited.

Long ago she had written him. A letter it was. He thought maybe a long letter. More than one page, anyway, he thought, long ago. He'd lost the letter. And forgotten. Mostly forgotten what it had said. But there was one thing.

One thing he remembered. *And*, she'd said, *it's not real.*

He remembered the *And* and everything.

And he knew that.

And he did not.

What was real, anyway?

She would not do anything. All right. She had become nothing. He was aware of that. Of course, he'd become nothing as well. But a little more, a little higher order of nothing than her.

But he was thinking of her. As the Toy Lady perhaps or maybe as the Whiskey Gal, true.

He was certain she was not thinking of him. Never gave him a thought. Not the slightest thought.

He knew. He knew how the world, which is only the world, you know, splits, and how the world, you know, is so small, and, you know, no world at all.

Yes, and THE PROBLEM OF LOVE.

Oh no, he thought.

He knew it was not there. He knew it was not coming.

Anything.

If he wanted something, he'd have to make it.

Make it. The notion seemed peculiar now. Retrospective, perhaps.

He had feared at one time people were spying on him. Long long ago. Now he knew no one paid any attention. He was insignificant. He was comic. He was sad.

He was a clown.

Certainly she had understood what he had not understood.

Hadn't everyone?

Back then he claimed his real name was not his name. He told everyone it was something else.

He would he'd decided have to make whatever he wanted himself.

Why, he might have to carve it out of something. That would be one way.

Or lightly, delicately, sketch it. That might be another.

It seemed to him he was always positing the existence of this or that and then working to make some rough approximation of it.

Certainly it seemed that way. If it was real. That is, if that was the way it really was.

Why the necessity of the Whiskey Gal? Couldn't she just as well be the Gin Gal?

Perhaps not just as well.

And.

He had thought he would have a life. A mental life. He had thought he would have thoughts. Thought. Consistent thought.

A body of thought.

He had thought that.

It had seemed important to him at the time.

Now he had begun to think his old friends were not in contact anymore because his old friends were dead.

Although he believed he would have heard if that were the case. He was not sure how he might have heard, only *that* he would have heard.

He was isolated and had to *imagine* himself a part of a community of the like-minded.

And then to imagine himself in perfect isolation.

Always the *must* of self. Of things.

He could stop.

He told himself that. Stop whenever he wanted. At any time.

Yes, the clock ticked.

Yes, time ran on.

Why wouldn't it? Why shouldn't it?

He made things. He could not stand to have things like the things he made, things made by others, in his house.

Was he alone in that?

Would she ever do anything?

He knew it did not matter. All that remained, really, was an endless, pointless conversation with himself.

There was an end to a thing.

He knew that.

My 40th Birthday Party

I am a big man, six feet two, 220 pounds, and while not the giant I aspired to be, big enough to be thankful for my height and girth. At work, people often greet me by calling me *big guy* or *chief*. I leave it to you to decide if a smaller, neater man, a man who did not bump into things with his large feet and have to constantly re-tuck his shirt, would be similarly greeted. There is, I know, a certain clumsy menace in my movements that alarms people or puts them at ease, as appropriate.

Even excess has its limits, and as the day approached, I harbored no illusions about aging and its probable effects on even a body as highly comfortable as my own. I noticed my vision going, especially where fine print was concerned, the letters blurring, fading, the sentences unraveling before my eyes. And spelling, all the spellings I thought correct were now inexplicably wrong, though I took this for a mental, as opposed to a bodily, failing, as if the two could be opposed.

I wondered was I wearing smooth.

At home, of course. In my off hours, of course.

At work, the technology developed by the state to create the super state sat on my desk in its latest consumer application.

And it was not all smooth or threatening a smooth anonymity. My teeth hurt, and when I yawned, my jaw spasmed, leading me to believe that I was, in fact, grinding them (my teeth) again in my sleep. Blotches, reddish blotches, appeared on my skin, and these blotches did not hurt or itch, these blotches didn't do anything, and it was well known that the ones that don't do anything, or more correctly, that the ones that initially appear not to do anything, were the most dangerous by far. There were also the bumps. Little, granular bumps on my upper arms. I could not tell whether these bumps hurt or not, for I, in all honesty, picked at them, and that hurt.

Again, I knew well as the day, *"the big day"* as Gloria called it, approached, the state of myself and the likely gloomy promise of my future. To assert otherwise or to accept those assertions from others, such as, say, Gloria, would be to lie profoundly, or to, as badly, embrace a profound lie, and I will accede to neither act.

But the party—well, was there anything wrong with a little celebration to mark the occasion? Wasn't that, a little celebration, what we were all agreed we needed to stave off the sterility of our commodified existence?

You knew she took my picture.

You knew she planned to take a lot of pictures at the party.

And she would it seemed to me, go along in good humor with any sort of party I wanted to have. In spite of all the years Gloria and I have been together, in spite of our remarkable closeness, in spite of our genial agreement about how to conduct our lives, I was shy, a bit reluctant to express my desires, for we were two radically different people, and there were elements of each that remained incomprehensible to the other.

I have never asked Gloria if she shares this sense; I take it for granted that she does. That she must. For mustn't everyone?

My tastes, in any event, were not so much aberrant as vulgar. Should not the theme of a party marking the incipient failure of the body recognize, or at least allude to, the adult pleasures of the flesh? It seemed to me that any such party should include pornographic videos, barrels of fried chicken, and hundreds of Budweiser tall boys. Vulgar, yes, but fun, and maybe more importantly, American, and why not enjoy the superficial pleasures of the most vigorous popular culture on the face of the earth, this cornucopia of nearly innocent and damned tasty fare?

That, roughly, was the party as I envisioned it.

A few days before we were to call people about the party—not many—the stray sibling and a handful of old friends—we went out to the superstore to do some bulk shopping, and there we saw something strange. A man in a vaguely Tyrolean outfit was playing a barrel organ and singing.

Somewhere in the world
The money goes round:

You'd best be sure
It comes to your town . . .

I looked for banners or some other indication that this was part of a larger promotion or fair, some little fucking costume drama like everything else, but there were none. I asked Gloria if she knew anything about this—she is sometimes more attuned to shopping events than I—but she had heard nothing of it. When we left the store with our industrial-sized cart of staples, the man was still there, singing to the same tune.

Sooner or later the devil comes round.
He'll take you out if you're not in the ground.

For some reason, I found the presence of this fellow deeply disturbing. Although we had discussed the party and had a rough plan for it, I was wavering. I was not sure that a party, any party, was altogether appropriate.

That night, I drank some wine, three or four glasses, with dinner. After dinner, I had four beers I found in the refrigerator. When the beer was gone, I started in on the Scotch. It seemed to me I drank almost half a bottle of Scotch after the beer and wine. I went to take a pill then, but the pill caught in my throat, and I gagged. Then I vomited up the pill and all.

The next morning I had bacon and eggs, hoping a big breakfast would make me feel better, not only physically, but psychologically as well.

My spiritual healer—well, he was supposed to appear to me in a dream, wasn't he—was nowhere to be found.

Still, when I went to drink from my big mug of iced tea at the breakfast table, the tea tasted like Scotch.

I hauled the paper bags of recyclables, that snapshot of our consumer waste, out to the curb as I did every week. I noticed the bottle bag was full of bottles and that there was a large green wine bottle—a jug really—that took up a great deal of room. The reason for that big bottle was that the wine, what had remained in the bottle, had gone bad. Air got into the bottle, so the wine had turned to vinegar. So we had to pour it out.

I thought, Oh Jesus, not the wine and vinegar.

I told her then, or if not then, shortly thereafter, that there would be no party.

That night, she kissed me and said I tasted like bacon. Being a barbarian, I assumed I gave off the faint scent of rancid butter.

And on my birthday, I sat drinking Scotch on the patio, and I heard Gloria, inside the house, exclaim flatly to herself or to the telephone or to the ceiling or to the TV—The People's Republic of Nothing.

My wife believed, perhaps, in the mediacy of history.

I, in the dark, peered dimly into my dark glass.

What could drinking teach me now?

Communication

Maybe if she would spare him the doxology. Start there he would tell her. Spare him and spoil what? Tell her he could not be more pleased if he had received a postcard that said Fuck You. Because there were some things she did not know. The social order and the end of privacy for example. At the end now—now at the end one was likely to be surrounded by strangers ending almost publicly. Not how anyone imagined it. Surrounded in some hellish room with the TV on God knows what. Intubated. How about that?

What could she say to that?

The Isle of the Sighted. Never heard of that.

Isle of the Blind, yes.

What? she had said.

One, he said.

One or the other he'd meant but obviously no point saying that.

He could write her a hate letter.

He did not believe he had ever written a hate letter.

Besides, it was all email now.

Had received plenty of hate email in the course of his work.

He could not understand what her pantheon was.

And birds.

Something is going to come from a bird and kill you, the TV said.

Death by bird: the bird brought it.

A siren in the night.

A collapse in the night.

A dropped glass. Glass overturned. Room empty, mostly dark. One lamp burning.

Some forced comedy of the moment in the forced comedy of the day. All the pretty vanities each by each. The construct one conducted. That public creation.

Privacy only perhaps in one's grief though he'd heard the celebrity on the radio. The celebrity described in great detail the agonizing death of the celebrity's young sister.

Something to trade on.

Something to trade with.

Splitting out his selves and making those selves enact a story of who the celebrity was. How it was done. Narrative self-explanatory, prefabricated so the listeners' reactions could be wholly predicted.

Right response implied also a wrong response.

The freedom of the known.

Not worth contemplating.

Movie based on a cartoon which was based on a video game which was based on a cereal box.

What he said to that. Nothing he said to that.

She quoted that movie.

To him.

The Bottle Game

Jug, jug, she said.

I was not inclined to reply. She raised her eyebrows as if to inquire did I take her meaning. I averted my eyes, which, as much as anything, answered her question.

First I had been censured at work for looking at pornography on the web. Apparently, it was company time. Company time and a company machine and company electricity. As well, they told me there were ethical and liability issues.

I had been in my office with my door locked locked locked.

As part of the censure they took my office away and gave me a work space in the middle of a large, open room. The people at the other work spaces could see me at mine and vice-versa. I was on display, as it were.

She knew all about it and had asked was I not embarrassed.

Should I have been ashamed?

Curiosity and biology had got the better of me, but I hardly felt that I was alone in this.

Later it took on some implications.

She wanted to know all about everything it seemed, yet she would berate me with great enthusiasm if I told her any thing that she felt was the wrong thing. I, of course, had no possible way to know what was right and what was wrong. And yet her desire to hear seemed to border on obsession. I suspected she believed that there was some mystery which could be unraveled by my speech, but if there were, it was a mystery to me.

Of course it was someone's idea, but I don't know who came up with the idea that we play the bottle game. I knew that I did not suggest such a thing. It would not be at all like me to suggest such a thing. Think about it, yes, but to verbalize it? That was, it seemed quite clearly to me, beyond my ken.

We had heard of the alleged dangers, and certainly we'd paid them no mind. The great surprise for me was the enthusiasm with which she embraced the game with all its complicated rituals and, at times, frankly, demanding format. But we were entirely at play for an hour or two each evening after I returned from my work space and for longer on weekends. It seemed a diversion perhaps or the only activity that could grant us release, no matter how temporary, from the banal concerns of our temporal existence.

Later there were some growing concerns.

I would like to report that I played with a skill that was phenomenal, that no one would have played or even could play the way I played. And it is true, I played with what seemed to me to be considerable success, and there were times, to be strictly honest, when I felt as though everything was unfolding completely naturally, when I was in complete harmony with the play, when it seemed as though I were a natural with an almost supernatural talent for the bottle game. But, alas, is it not equally true that everyone or nearly everyone who plays has similar, if not identical, feelings? The same self appraisal?

There is frequently a caution of balance. This caution of balance is so frequently offered as to be a commonplace although one might question whether the multitudes who so frequently offer it actually observe it. Besides, was it not those multitudes we wished to escape? After all, when we played, we felt in the play that we had separated ourselves in some fundamental way from the mass irregardless of how many others might also *even at that moment* be playing the identical, save for minor individual preferences and variations, game.

Sometimes at my work station, I dreamed of the bottle game and was lost in my thoughts. The spreadsheets on my work surface were meaningless then: black on white, numbers and letters spinning free of context.

However, I was forced, as others have, to reluctantly conclude that the bottle game changed nothing. Little, of course, changes anything. Except time. And tried though I might to think nothing of it, time came inevitably around.

They gave me my office back. There was no explanation offered for this. Even my computer was returned; however, it goes without saying that I no longer had internet access and that internet access was unlikely to ever return to me.

Not that that any longer held my interest.

And I was becoming weak in a way I had not understood was coming. Tired to the point of exhaustion. I sometimes dreamed of exhaustion, and this was new to me. And though they had installed me again in my office, this installation filled me with doubt and fear.

It might be that this meant that they were watching and waiting for an excuse to finish me off.

She seemed weary too, and with my knowledge that things were slipping at work, that I needed to rest and attempt to regain my focus and status there, it was almost as though by some unspoken agreement we virtually abandoned the bottle game.

There was the occasional perfunctory play, but in the larger sense, that part of our lives was over. For how could we play to the neglect of all else when the bottle game was what?

What was it but the promise of everything?

A promise, of course, impossible to fulfill.

What else was there, however, for us, when the day is like the night?

Crow

One day he would throw his shoes away and they would be gone. That was one message. And a crow is black. And there are those healthy men who heartily eat big dinners and something sticks somewhere and cough, cough, cough, they're dead. That fellow who retched, choked, vomited, and died.

He did not want to beg for mercy, but he knew he might.

He knew he would.

He could not buy enough guns to save himself.

The installer came to his house to install the new equipment. The installer was fanatically loyal to his employer. At the first suggestion that any equipment might work equally well, the offended installer angrily corrected him. The installer seemed a man who knew no anxiety. Absolutely sure of himself, the installer knew only what he knew and knowing only that knew his worldview complete.

The installer was exactly what the installer said he was.

He could not say as much.

The party of making things work was working on making things work by engineering the present as nothing but what it is. He suspected in their secret work areas party members were creating a precise replica of the status quo that would continue into the foreseeable future.

The installer would fit with them.

As would the crow.

They were sending no message forward, but what need was there for them to send one forward?

Or he could not receive the message. The installer installed the network he could not understand. The network and the understanding of the network were the same thing. To not understand the network in the way he did not understand the network was to be outside the message that allowed one to partake fully of the network.

He'd be a dull spectator, he understood.

For example, he *paid*. He did not *profit*. If one *paid* one did not know what one was paying for. Every time he *paid*, he lost.

The chronic nature of it bothered him.

He did not make the precise calculation of loss.

The installer could. The installer no doubt kept records that mattered. The installer did not put off inconvenient or unpleasant tasks. The installer took the world as it was and installed the network to make it more that way.

The installer would eat the meat of the world, and, if lucky, he might be left some scrap of cold fish like the seagulls.

Or the crows.

Film

She emailed him that she had chosen to participate in the great renunciation.

Couldn't she have simply told him at supper?

He was, theoretically, all for giving things up.

This was some time after the big game. During the big game, he had sat there drinking malt liquor and cheering while she and the children watched in confusion and disgust.

—You're going to find out, he told her, that your wonder machine causes brain cancer.

But it was an empty threat, and both of them knew it although he was reluctant to believe it. The way she did things, said things, in particular, so casually, so off-handedly. All of this, he was sure, had started much earlier. For example, the invitation from his work to the holiday party said his name and *companion*. *Companion*, he had never thought of her that way.

He had to think back, and when he thought back, he thought he remembered something he had long forgotten. A desire. Hard to put into words. He had been puzzled by what he did not know about her—he had wanted to know everything. He wanted to know everything she thought and why she thought it and how she thought it and of course he wanted to control it. He had observed her. Talked to her. Questioned her. Sometimes he had imagined himself a scientist studying her with a purposeful and sterile objectivity.

That was long ago, he felt.

Lately, he had been losing things. He lost the little aluminum flashlight he kept in the glove compartment. He needed it for something and looked for it and it was not there. If that was not lost, what was lost? And he lost a pen, his good pen, the roller ball he kept in his shirt pocket at work. Vanished. That was a two-dollar pen.

So he was all alone.

He would go to China which was beneath the sea and live there alone. What else could he do but seek solace in religion, an idea he had long ago rejected, but that now struck him with a dim hope, for did not he, of all people, deserve solace?

Maybe, he considered, that mystery he had seen in her so long ago was not in her at all, maybe it was something, some kind of untieable knot in his head.

If he could give up trying to understand, only admit that it was and would forever remain incomprehensible. Maybe if he could not seek solace, he could try to find some comfort. He was not sure how to go about that. Where did you start—make a list of things that made you comfortable?

It was this constant talk talk talk. These words in his head. Though shutting them off was not much of an option, maybe there was a way to make them say, do, something else. Sing him a pretty song instead of interrogating him in this hopeless dialogue.

Then he was walking into work and there in the slush in the parking lot lay a perfectly good pen. Not his pen, though. This was a Japanese ballpoint that sold for a dollar, maybe a little more. Did he have to pick it up? He could afford to buy a pen, a thousand pens, if he wanted to. He did not have to pick pens off the slushy ground; he could afford not to.

He left the pen where it lay.

His desire of many years ago had dissipated certainly, and it was only a memory now. A memory that he could, occasionally, catch full force and truly feel. It seemed, though, that he had gradually abandoned his desire, that desire which was so compulsive it had seemed an inextricable part of him, some core element of his personality.

Over the years he had realized, to his great embarrassment, that the two of them, him and her, were much the same. This realization was a bitter disappointment to him.

She had seemed to him to be so much more than himself, and, in retrospect, than herself, as though she embodied some profound mystery, the revelation of which held for him a terrible and salvatory promise. When he realized they were more or less alike, that promise disappeared. He was troubled by what he did not know about himself. There was something he was sure, probably something bad and plenty of it. And to think it was, at best, the same for her.

Then he found his pen. It had been on the dresser the whole time.

Then he rented a film. The film was on video. There were fantastic scenes in the film in which the beautiful actress descended a rope from great height at a great speed. It was an operatic adrenal release. Later there was a spectacle, a parade from the theatre, that featured the beautiful actress.

He had seen several of her films.

She had become over the years a symbolic figure to him, emptied of quotidian humanity. She was not a person and certainly not the person she was, in his mind.

Like a beautiful dream this created desire could not be captured.

Could it be said to truly exist?

He would not realize, or did, at some level he was looking at her and seeing not the actress but the other, his companion, who many years before had offered him her grab bag at a party.

Catch and Release

It was the pin prick prick. Sometimes his knee, sometimes his side. Or his abdomen, though there not so sharply. He knew it was nothing, but he was afraid. He was afraid because he thought he had heard, or maybe read, somewhere, that there was a horrible neurological disease that usually began in middle age and initially manifested itself as the prickly sensation of random pin pricks. But he thought that if this were true, and he suspected that he had, as usual, got the details wrong, and it was not true, there would be a lot of pin pricks. Not one every three or four days but thousands, millions. They would be constant. Massive. Debilitating. Chronic.

So he was okay, but soon, it would be something, some chronic this or constant that. That's the way it was for everybody, and there was no use trying to defeat reality.

In Colorado, they released the pretty lynx. It made the news, and the paper had a picture of the lynx shoulder-deep in snow. Apparently they were getting rare, at least in that part of the state, so the officials released some captive lynx in hopes they'd repopulate the wild. Toni told him the lynx weren't extinct there. She told him, too, that the released animals were wearing radio collars so the fish and game people could track them.

Probably they were losing habitat to development. Maybe they were hunted too. More likely trapped. They had beautiful fur; there was no disputing that. He hoped, as he supposed most people did, that the lynx would do fine out there. Colorado, after all, the mountains, you know, forests and streams and so forth—there was a place for all that. But then the farmers and the ranchers—they might not be too happy about having another predator in the area.

Toni, though, was so excited about these wildcats. She was hoping there would be reports about where they were going. Well, where could they go?

They'd run around the forest, right? Even if there were a graphic on TV, that graphic would show what—dotted lines on a topo map?

It was forty degrees, and the ice was melting on the back of the house, that drip, drip, drip, and though the sky was a heavy, moist gray, the air smelled spring-like, and though the garage was cluttered with the old weight set and beer crates and potting soil, pots, tools, the broken lawn-mower—he had seen something scurrying, he thought, in there the other night—he thought it was a field mouse taken up winter residence, and he wasn't sure what to do about it or whether he needed to do anything about it, for it might be best simply to leave the thing alone—in spite of all this, he recognized for a moment something inside him, something he felt, physically felt inside his chest, and it was, it was a feeling, and it was a feeling, a familiar feeling, for a moment, of *possibility*.

He got into the car.

The feeling went away.

Today was the conference. The conference was, in theory, better than going to the office, except that instead of going out to the industrial park, he had to go downtown to the big hotel, which was not in itself a bad thing, but there were the traffic and the parking. However, the hotel had a ramp. But the ramp was expensive. He would, though, he could, put in for reim-bursement. If the ramp were not full, because if the hotel ramp were full, he'd have to find another ramp nearby. He knew, roughly, where there was one, but that rough knowledge was the problem: With all the construction and one-way streets downtown, he was not sure where to enter or how to get to the entrance.

The conference was about The Future.

Maybe it was good they were sending him, or maybe they picked him because he was the most expendable. They told him to go and hear what the experts had to say about the future. He knew enough to know that the experts would have dramatic predictions about the future and its atten-dant challenges. That was their job. He never believed those predictions. Sure, there might be some technological advances, but it took awhile for the effects of anything to ripple out, and what change he really had to worry about would come incrementally.

He knew his point of view was no longer popular.

No one believed in increments now; they were all waiting for the revolutions that really were not revolutions at all.

At the stoplight, he noticed four or five fat, black crows in the bare trees. One good thing about this thaw, most of the sand and salt had run with the water to the sides of the street.

He got to the hotel, and there was plenty of space in the ramp, so much that he found a space on the third level. This was unprecedented. He could not remember a time when he'd gotten a space in a downtown ramp on a level lower than the fifth, and usually he ended up on the roof. At least then he got to look out over downtown.

He took the elevator down to the lobby. The desk clerk had a heavy German accent. That struck him as curious; who would come all the way from Germany to don the maroon and brass uniform of a desk clerk? But the clerk told him that the conference had been moved although the clerk could not explain why the conference had been moved. The conference had been moved to a community college in the suburbs, that little satellite of learning, which was, ironically, less than two miles from his work.

He got in the car and made a half-hearted attempt at convincing the ramp attendant he should not have to pay for the twelve minutes the car was in the ramp, but the attendant said it was ramp policy that every ticket had to be paid, so he paid and got out of there, out of downtown, onto the freeway.

He drove five miles above the speed limit.

A black car came up fast behind him. He was in the middle lane, and the other lanes were clear—plenty of room to pass him. Of course the car was right up on him. It tailgated him for about a mile. He neither sped up nor slowed down.

The car pulled quickly out and passed him on the right.

He glanced at the driver, a greased-back-hair-headed hipster, some thirty-year-old, low-life, petty business type, leaning back in his cheap suit, one hand on the wheel, as he zipped about in his black Cougar.

Cougar—that said it all.

He took his normal exit.

Across from the cinderblock strip mall that was kitty corner from the cinderblock gas station, a cinderblock minimart was going up. The community college, he realized, was made of cinderblock too. Here he was, beyond doubt, in cinderblock land.

There was plenty of parking, acres and acres of lot in front of the college. And signs. A big banner over the door and signs on stands inside, all directing the conferencees to the auditorium for the conference. He stopped at the folding table to pick up his packet and nametag. The woman there told him things had just started.

The seats in the back were all taken, so he had to go to the middle of the auditorium to find a place.

The speaker stood at a podium on stage. A PowerPoint presentation was going. The screen was covered with statistics.

—Ever try to throw out a garbage can? The speaker said.

The audience laughed.

The speaker nodded. —That's right, we all know it's almost impossible.

So it always came back to garbage. Of course, this was simply a metaphor that led into the detailed version of the future. He thought dully of his own future. That didn't take long. Then he thought of the past. The speaker spoke energetically for a long time. That was the speaker's job.

To sit and listen with apparent interest—that was his job.

He thought about the past. He had quit smoking three years before and now it was like a familiar itch; of a sudden, he wanted a cigarette. He felt the urge to make a list of every brand of cigarette he'd ever smoked and then to get a cigarette of each brand and smoke every one. He could feel the blue smoke coming out of his lungs.

How long had it been, he wondered, since he had been in a room where the air was blue with smoke?

Three hours later, they had a break. Twenty minutes before lunch. He did not think a place had been reserved for him at lunch.

Best anyway to get out.

Always best to in any way get out.

Somehow he got turned around and ended up walking almost the block-long length of the building. There was so much concrete, so many cinderblocks. Every so often, although not, it seemed, at regular intervals, there were built-ins, concrete benches with fabric-covered cushions, these little niches set in odd angles of the strange building, presumably for students to relax, sit down, take a break, talk. He came around a turn, and there, sitting on one of the benches, was an old man, white bearded, his mouth hanging open. He nodded to the old man, but the old man did not see him. Clearly, the old man did not see him. The old man's expression was pained, distracted, pained and distracted at the same time.

He realized he was going the wrong way—this building was like a maze—and turned sharply and walked quickly away from the old man. Was that it? To sit on the thin, soiled cushions of the concrete bench and contemplate your doom in the common area of the community college?

He couldn't get the car going fast enough. Some soft rain began to fall. Later it would fall freezing and the roads would be treacherous. The old man wasn't all of it. He did not know how to describe, what to say, if he were to say, to try to describe it to Toni. It was all of it.

Everybody tried to describe it. Everybody wanted to capture it in a word. That was the match everybody lost, but tried, why not? What else? He drove to the other exit, the work exit. At least the area was all right. The developers had left some trees, some ponds, some little clumps of brush that suggested woods, even if they weren't woods. There was one tree, though, a big, old elm that had blown down in a storm a couple months before. This was right by the roadside, not far from his work. Once, there had been a lot of elms around, but not anymore. That was okay. A tree was the past, the woods, the forest, all that time, any time. He went by the tree, and as he passed, he slowed down. It looked like they'd do something with that tree, like they'd saw it up and haul it away. But looking at it now, it looked like someone had only sawed off some of the limbs—the ends of the limbs.

In a wood-burning culture, he thought, that tree would be long gone.

But he knew this was an oil-burning culture. That seemed more modern. Then again, was it more modern to dig up the oldest black stuff under everything, the stuff that was alive long ago, and then to quickly burn it quickly all up?

Culture

One day everything in the world was based on a comic book.

Clotilde wanted to see a movie, so he took her. A gangster movie. Even by gangster movie standards, the movie unreal. He remarked on it.

It's based on a graphic novel, Clotilde said.

He was not surprised.

Why not?

He'd long ago surrendered his argument with the culture.

Culture? Who believed that?

The community college in his community was reading a common book. All the students and the teachers were supposed to read the same book and members of the community were encouraged to read it too, and when everyone had read it, the college was going to sponsor a gathering in celebration of the common book and the common reading of it.

Clotilde told him about the book.

He said he'd never heard of it.

It was a famous graphic novel everyone had heard of. It dealt with important themes of history and culture and identity.

Clotilde told him that.

What was he supposed to do—apologize?

He did not want anything.

He tried not to want anything.

He told himself to try not to want anything.

Life was what, an expectancy for him of, seventy-eight years.

He was forty-nine.

Maybe take off ten, twelve years for all those cigarettes he used to smoke.

No one needed to explain.

Clotilde wanted to see the Egyptian show.

At the museum.

He'd lost interest in Egyptian things when he was a child. When he found out the Mummy was not anything like real mummies.

Still she wanted to go.

He would have liked to see Beckmann and Grosz if he looked at pictures but those kinds of things would not come to his community.

He did not say anything.

Who was he to talk?

While she looked at the Egyptian show, he had a fancy coffee in the fancy coffee shop. It was good. He went to the museum book store.

Not looking for anything but who knew.

Many clever toys there and more books on more subjects than he would have predicted.

Then.

He picked it up. Collection. Comic strips about sex. Like a porn movie in black and white, paper and ink.

Well done.

They wanted $24.00 for it.

She was looking at the Egyptian things.

He was forty-nine.

And still he had no money.

Science

To send an idea by way of wire he told Burkett was not to give the wire ideas.

Burkett tongued his broken tooth and continued to read a stolen airline magazine.

Would you, he asked Burkett, gorge on an animal whose flesh might destroy you?

This one the meat killed him.

This one the car wreck.

The other down the flood it was said but he knew better.

Knew a woman once, he said, and I wanted to tell her to have a little clarity. Clarity, it seemed had fallen out of the language at that time.

Burkett styled himself the visionary futurist.

Machines without will Burkett dreamed of yet machines intelligent.

Intelligence without will he knew from some other context.

Was there an in and an out?

How would Burkett understand the phrase what a house was.

Elegance of the machine the elegance of command and execution in perfect merger but elegant as well in construction and function. Obvious from Burkett's description or inference or projection.

Burkett unable to understand a language is only the language.

And what the fuck?

Obligation to be free of it only the beginning. The beginning of the rootless drifter. Though it did not—could not—matter.

Rooted, unrooted, drifting or not, a victim in the wake in any case.

Burkett could not invent a way out.

No matter how completely he envisioned the totality of technological solution.

Blinded, they say.

Unable to see, perhaps.

Everything he hated in himself so clear to himself.

Punished with savage conscience or with savage conscience punished.

The only eloquent thought in accusatory mode.

He had to be what he was and what he was not with equal facility and see himself, if at all, in some negative definition or relief.

Burkett claimed he was going blind. Don't you see it, Burkett said, a blind man could see it.

He held up the bottle to Burkett and said, Want some correction fluid?

He passed a guy in a liquor store entryway. A guy he used to drink with. Guy he'd heard had gone to treatment. The guy did not recognize him or the guy was not the guy.

Then he remembered that guy was dead.

All engendered in a moment now gone.

Time went backwards and forwards or the other way around.

This was not true.

Or it was not quite that way.

Burkett accepted and adored storage. Everything would be stored in the future for the future. Nothing would ever disappear.

Nothing.

Like a place where maybe you were high and there was something going on in the back and the light the way it was and you were high and you knew there were some guns in the back.

That would never disappear.

He wanted to move away from life.

All his life he wanted this.

Burkett wanted everything recorded which seemed to mean to make everything more everything than everything already was.

It was said.

For a reason.

Because that was the way it was.

Burkett's cosmology worse than an acceptance, an enthusiasm.

Were any of Burkett's friends dead?

Never heard Burkett mention a person in other than a business or technical context.

People.

Building the structures for the structures' sake.

Shirt

Molly wanted him to take her to the museum.

—Do you know what a museum is for? He said.

—Of course I know what a museum is. Everybody knows what a museum is.

—Is for, he said, not is.

—This museum has Indians, she said.

—Indians, he said.

Jesus Christ, he thought.

Of course he had always wanted to go out West, to drive through the West and see all of the West he had seen in movies and pictures and television programs, for he was, after all, an American, and it seemed, along with his desire, it was almost his obligation to at least want to see the West, even if he never really got around to seeing the West. Not this year maybe, but if not this year, next year, or the year after that.

He was wearing a flannel shirt, and she objected to that. She said it was too early in the year to wear flannel.

—Do I have to remind you, he said, that flannel is made out of cotton?

—You can wear all the flannel shirts you want, she said. You're still a civil servant.

—I had these shirts before I had the job, he said.

He lit a cigarette.

—Go ahead, she said. Smoke. It won't protect you.

—I didn't think that was the idea, he said

He had been asked to a house. A function for a woman at work who was having a baby. Men and women. The women looked at the baby presents, the men drank beer, everybody ate. Impressive patio, and they had not scrimped when it came to the lawn furniture. They had a family room as well with a big-screen TV. No game that day, unfortunately. The men left to themselves on that patio. The game exhausted, work exhausted, they had to talk about something, so they all sat around and talked about the things they wanted. One wanted a boat, another wanted a satellite dish, a third wanted a swimming pool. His turn came, not that it was an organized kind of thing, but the conversation came around to him, and he had to say something, but for a moment he couldn't think of anything, well, there was a bass boat, he wanted a bass boat, but Ned had already talked about boats, so he said, and it surprised him when it came out, he said, —I always wanted to go trekking in the Himalayas. You know, Bhutan, Nepal?

Then it was somebody else's turn to talk.

But that was not what he wanted. He really did not want anything. That's what he'd tell Molly, that he had everything he needed and he did not want anything else.

—Oh, she said, you want something.

She thought he wanted a cabin. A log cabin with a stone fireplace in the woods on a cold, clear lake. It was true that he had a book about building log cabins, and occasionally he'd leaf through an outdoor magazine, and he had a catalog of plans from a company that built log houses, but those things did not add up to anything. He was curious. He was interested in things, in what things were and how things worked. Why shouldn't he be? With all there was in this wide world, why not try, try at least, to take an interest in a few of the myriad of things extant? But to actually want a cabin, to forgo the abstraction of interest for the reality of physical ownership, that was beyond his interest, that was farther, much, much farther, than he was prepared to go.

Then there was all the work. All the maintenance. There was the constant risk of burglary. Of arson. Of vandalism. There was the obligation, the sense of obligation that, having invested in a cabin, one had to then spend all his free time at the cabin to recoup the investment. There was the travel time. There was the further obligation to speak sincerely, almost wistfully, to others about the cabin, about how one loved the cabin and how one had had a wonderful time at the cabin and how one could not wait to get back to the cabin and how one could not wait to retire to the cabin.

That would not be a cabin; that would be a new life.

No one ever mentioned dying there.

Perhaps it was implied.

And there was money. Though everyone was always busy pretending otherwise, money was at the bottom of most things.

He couldn't afford it.

He could do it, maybe, if he emptied his retirement account. That was the only way.

And then what? Retire to the cabin and gnaw the bark off the trees?

He wasn't going to any museum, and for the moment, it looked like he wasn't driving out West or anywhere else.

Billings was dead.

Not that he had known Billings other than to say hello to him at work, but Billings was dead, and, aside from the obvious tragedy, that screwed up the entire vacation rotation.

He had mixed feelings. On the one hand, Billings must have known that he would screw up the rotation and he may well have acted deliberately. On the other hand, Billings clearly had some worries, some problems, some profound troubles that claimed his attention and maybe left him unable or unwilling to rationally contemplate the consequences of his actions.

—What he did was, Ned said, he ate that stop leak stuff for the car.

—And it killed him, Ned said.

—How could Billings do that? He said. He wasn't a kid.

—He saw something in it. That neat little package maybe.

After the funeral, the goddamned game was blacked out. Some funeral anyway. The priest was up there talking about chemical imbalance. Brain chemicals. How was the priest supposed to be talking about that?

He had got the malt liquor and the frozen chicken wings on the way home and no game. He picked up a magazine and punched the remote.

The magazine fell open to a piece on grizzly bears. There was a hair, a big hair of moderate length, stuck to the magazine. He picked the hair off and dropped it, hoping it was one of Molly's, and not some grimy, curious postal worker's. On TV, they were climbing the unconquered peaks of Antarctica in the name of adventure. Cold and spacious and vacant. All there in three dimensions.

It wasn't even worth putting the wings in the microwave.

He had tried, he had gone to the gun show, and not having the price of a rifle, he had bought himself a Bowie knife.

So it was made in Pakistan? So what?

Molly had taken to calling him poor substitute.

First she left, then she came back, and people were still throwing trash on his lawn. Today it was a cigarette package with a brand he'd never heard of, a brand he wasn't sure existed.

—Why can man see colors? Molly asked him that.

—So he can hunt, he told her.

—Why aren't you out hunting? She said.

Oh, they'd been back and forth. No surprise there. At least not anymore, but there had been a time in living memory when it was considered good to eat and good to eat a lot. He was a big man, and she could say what she wanted, but she could not deny the truth in that.

—Clearly, she said, one should be a hunter or a mendicant. What other option could make sense?

Once she started in, once she really got going like this, he knew he could not stop her. Now if he were to wear the Bowie knife on his belt, then he could understand there might be objections. But what really could she ask of him? He too wanted to go and see a palace of wonders, but strictly speaking there was no such place, and the closest thing to it, if not found in the stadium, would have to be the mall. After all, they were not children.

Mounted on a plaque in the den, if he had a den, that Bowie knife would look pretty damn good.

This, it seemed to him, was no time for reflection.

He cut himself on the pop-up lever on a soda can. He was at work and he was bringing the can down from his mouth after he had taken a drink and he turned, half-turned, in his chair and somehow he scraped the can, which was in his right hand, against his left forearm and cut himself a little nick in the flesh there. Well, he had to go on as though nothing had happened—he was in a meeting—but he pressed a kleenex to the wound to stop the bleeding although the bleeding wasn't much and it wasn't what worried him. What worried him were two things. It seemed like he couldn't do anything lately without cutting himself, like he was getting clumsier and clumsier, and he was plenty clumsy to start off with, but now he was always cutting himself or banging into things or tripping over his own feet. The other thing was worse. He had heard about that flesh-eating bacteria, heard about it and seen the pictures on TV, and he could not get it out of his mind. He knew it was rare. Extremely rare. They said that. They said that and then they showed the pictures. And he knew the odds were infinitesimal that he would ever suffer from it. And he knew, in another way, really that it could not happen to him. But he thought about it. Every little scratch seemed to hurt more than scratches had before he, with every little scratch, contemplated the possibility of being eaten alive.

He had thought the city of the future was supposed to be like Japan where you could buy beer and pornography and oxygen from vending machines, but he had never figured on new or resurgent pathogens. Of course, in Japan they didn't have any cars either. None to speak of, anyway.

And what of that relatively modern invention, antisepsis?

He told Molly about the cut and the bacteria, and she said he was neurotic.

Neurotic? Did the word still have any credence? He meant, did anybody still use that word?

It was like when he told her he had decided to improve his vocabulary.

—Are you nuts? She said. Nobody does that anymore.

Now they had, it was a fact, chemical castration. He wondered if he could be chemically muted.

This was at the supper table. And what was it about this food? The slices of bread seemed like crackers, like wafers, and his beer can thimble-sized. He was a big man at the peak, for Christ's sake, of his strength. And he knew that peak would be brief and the precipitous decline quick and ugly, uglier than he could imagine.

He looked at his arm. The cut, the scab where he'd torn the skin, was shaped like a bird sitting on a limb. He had a scar where he had taken some stitches as a kid in the shape of a seven.

He went on, of course, seeing some possibility in himself. This despite the implacable boredom of day-to-day middle-class life.

He thought he should burn all the photographs of himself. Not at first, he hadn't thought that, but he was looking for the booklet that came with the lawnmower and told, showed, in fact, how to take the blade off and sharpen it, and instead he found an envelope full of black and white pictures Molly had taken, and in the envelope there were several of him, but one in particular, a side view, that somehow caught his rotting, misshapen teeth and the gray in his hair and made him look like, if not a dead man, a very sick man indeed. The teeth were not so much his fault, he felt. He felt it was mostly genetics, genetics and the fact that when he was younger money was a little tight and he had not gone to the dentist as often as he should have. He now understood that life reduced itself to a series of economic choices. Death did as well, if he pursued his line of thought.

But it was better to think of something else.

He thought his intention was to bring his Bowie knife to Jim Bowie's house in Washington, Louisiana, and there to have a priest bless it.

That made, didn't it, as much sense as going to some Indian museum?

Till in the fall one day as it grew cooler and cooler, he said —All right, all right, that's enough. Put on your coat and let's go.

He had been looking at an advertisement in the travel magazine he subscribed to. The magazine was full of ads for and stories about places he would never visit. Still, there were a lot of good pictures in that magazine. Pretty. The ad was for a resort in Bora Bora. Who would not want to go there, yet he was not certain he should want to go there. What about the Tibetans? They stayed where they were unless someone forced them out. You did not see them dreaming of Bora Bora just because some magazine featured photos of it.

Fall, and people had pumpkins on their porches. All right, he drove her over there as the leaves that hadn't fallen were still falling.

By thinking about things, you could understand them. He had heard that someplace. Maybe when he was a kid. It seemed almost like a kind of promise.

He stood before the glass case.

At least they had something sacred to go inside.

The guide moved them from case to case, the guide who didn't look like a guide. He looked like an angry man who might take an inordinate interest in how other people lived, this guide. The guide showed them the ghost shirt in the case and said that ghost shirts were always blue.

He knew all about ghost shirts.

—Ghost shirts, he said to Molly, were supposed to stop bullets. But they didn't work too good.

—You don't understand what you're saying, the guide said.

—The ghost shirt, the guide said, was not magical armor.

—The ghost shirt, the guide said, was a promise of redemption.

Aperture

He had a picture of himself and his wife at Graceland. The staff photographed the tourists as the tourists went in. At the end of the tour, he'd had the option of buying the photograph. Photographs. There were, he thought, various packages.

They were on vacation and though it seemed a little silly they'd taken the tour and he'd bought the picture.

It was cheaper than a T-shirt, he thought.

Once they'd snapped the picture, they had him. That's why they took the picture up front. After all, how many times was he going to be there?

You could not get them to not take the picture; you were on their property, and you had to go by their rules if you wanted to take the tour.

All you could do was refuse to buy it.

Then—who knew—they threw the unbought pictures away, didn't they? What might they want with keeping them? If they wanted a picture of anyone who came through the gate, so what?

It was probably good for security.

A goddamned trinket, a tourist souvenir.

You know when they got home they did not really know what to do with it. What were they supposed to do, frame it and put it over the mantle?

They did not have a mantle.

It ended up in a box, he thought. One of those things you get that goes into a box as though it had been created to go into a box.

All those things you get on vacation.

He did not know where the box was. It was not as though he were looking for it. Some day, he supposed, they'd be going through boxes of old things, and they would find it.

His wife believed in the future when the planet was pretty much played out some people—the rich and powerful at least—would travel to another planet and colonize it.

The idea had been around for years.

He could not seriously subscribe to it.

She said she wanted to be transported to another world.

He—well—he could not see that.

She believed the plans were all drawn up. That seemed a little extreme. Any such plans would depend on technologies not yet developed even if they were already imagined. Or existed theoretically. The point was there was no practical way to do any of this yet. Someday maybe. But planned? One could not plan in a vacuum.

She never accounted for who would be left behind. Get her on that, and she changed the subject. Get anybody who believed in, who supported, some exodus of the chosen and the left behind, well, they just fell away, didn't they?

They were gone. Though they had not gone anywhere.

They ceased to be a concern.

It was all fantasy. Mythology. The mythology of insecurity, the mythology of science fiction, the mythology of redemption melded into a cheesy pop culture concept unworthy of itself.

A reflection of the general insecurity in the culture. That insecurity broadcast daily.

Do not be in a crowd.

Do not be alone.

Do not be in a confined environment with others.

Do not be out of reach of others.

All the truly useless instruction.

Like the constant call to acquire the useless.

He was not going to do anything about it. He was not against it. He only wanted to not hear it. He knew he had nothing to do with any of it and all of it had nothing to do with him.

If they left in spaceships, he'd be gone.

He knew that.

He was not so sure he would not just as soon be gone. Be among the gone.

You could get a kidney—a human kidney—for $30,000 US. He knew that. It was a fact, and he knew it for a fact. Not that anyone had planned that. People implemented it, true. And he'd heard some governments were involved. It was a function of the market. Everyone said the market was good. There was no market to migrate to another planet. Not yet. No other planet had been identified. Why couldn't she or wouldn't she understand that?

It was not like the movies, nothing like the movies about the world without humans, the world with only machines and aliens and stereotypically sweet children. The movies certainly asserted the world was that but the world was not that. Unless the assertion was that the world was not that.

He was not sure.

He knew the aliens and the machines were supposed to help the idealized children and then they were gone.

Whatever gone meant.

He hated those movies yet once they entered the culture they kept coming back, eternally recycled to squeeze every bit of possible profit from them. If nothing else, images to carry advertising as a host culture carries bacteria in a lab.

People used them. With nothing to bind them but an imagined history, those images were binding.

Records of things that did not happen.

That could not.

The ingestion of those images the history in itself.

He'd bought the picture. What kind of asshole wouldn't have bought the picture?

What kind of asshole would have?

He had seen a movie of brain surgery years before. The surgeon stimulated portions of the exposed brain and the patient spoke of apparently long-forgotten memories. He did not know if the theory demonstrated in the film had subsequently been discredited, but he believed parts of his brain could be manipulated. The guilt center, for example, could be manipulated as he manipulated it with beer and wine and bourbon.

The parts of his brain, he presumed, structured like the parts of any other human brain and manipulable by external stimuli systematically applied.

The media. The market.

Interchangeable.

Weren't all organs theoretically? Hadn't that been demonstrated? Stem cells, the plasticity of matter, his interchangeability. He was this and nothing as well.

So how gone was gone? Or, by leaving, where did one get?

The varieties of chaos to come—he did not know anything about what that was supposed to mean.

Apparently she wanted a story where something meant something. He did not believe in cars that ran on water or suppressed cancer cures or alien corpses in government storage.

—I don't believe in anything, he'd told her.

She said that was not true. He did not understand what it was she thought she meant.

One day they would open a box and find it and experience a moment of recognition. That recognition surprise and delight at the past. There could be no recognition of the future as it had yet to arrive though it might be a future where one was photographed or filmed everywhere—incessantly.

Weather

He claimed someone at the office pushed the political button on him.

The competing claim he'd pushed it on himself. And why would anyone do such a thing to himself but to clarify his continuing failure?

Away, he was alone.

Alone in his room, he feared God might not be protecting his home and his people as he wished God might. Outside his room, the hills and the trees. The forest and farther off, he believed, the water.

As though he had been placed here in the middle of all this nothing. Or forest. Or land.

Or water.

The others had gotten out of it and he was left in his room to wait until he could get out.

He knocked over the bottle. Crack of it hitting the table loud—echoing as though the room were empty.

The bottle did not break.

The terror one could be alone here for all the time he had.

Forest as far as he could see.

Every second relentless.

Dull ache in the whiskey.

She lonesome somewhere as he was here.

His city experiencing an increase in dementia. The ever-aggressive senior drivers. Depression on the rise, hanging like despair over the yards and family rooms.

The food in the stores appeared as other—as normal—food.

The exhausted love of the now in the cul-de-sacs.

The place itself suspect.

In his fantasy life, he was already in Thailand.

His daily life a slumber of responsibilities.

He was supposed to take things as they came and accept things for what they were.

He contemplated, as the desperate man will, the varieties of lust.

Delayed here against his will.

Everything was going backwards or everything was winding down.

And what was the difference and how could he tell it.

No reason to know.

Looked out and saw an army of greasy starlings on his front lawn. Week ago. Aggressive winged vermin.

Sometimes it was sunny.

Sometimes it was raining.

His long absence followed by his long silence.

His motives, he knew, were not pure. As that Wastrel Prince from that what was it story.

Not that it mattered.

Sometimes it was cloudy; he needed to remember that.

The one life. His. The one and only life. This.

Everything now could be expressed in a song. What other inefficient narrative worth pursuing?

He kept the lights off at home so he could see into the dark cul-de-sac.

A world neither true nor false.

He had nothing to do. Intentionally, he was given nothing to do. They were waiting for him to go, of course. That was why.

He like a guest that would not leave, exasperating, then annoying, then despised, finally hated.

Sometimes he saw something flit like a little bat on the periphery of his vision. A little bat that lived only in his head.

Why the Vampyre now?

A person could withdraw into himself though not permanently.

Correct.

At the meeting, he was asked to perform in the little piece. Nonsense. What was one to do? Pitched neither above nor below its audience but directly at it.

As this little exile.

Thought

He thought he could not get over anything, and he knew successful people got over everything and moved forward, for if one could not get over things, one could not move forward and be successful.

I can't seem to get over anything, he said.

You know, D said, people want some reassurance.

I know, he said.

People want, D said, that reassurance of meaning, of spirit. I'm not saying you have to be a darling.

I know I'm no darling, he said.

What I'm saying, D said, is you have to meet people somewhere. If people think you dislike them or disdain them, you're not going to get anywhere.

He hated D. It crossed his mind to kill D.

People, D said, want to trust you. They want you to allow them to think of you as a friend—someone who likes them or allows them to like you.

He could shoot D, but he did not have a gun.

If you don't start, D said, with that sense that a relationship is possible, then there is nothing to build on, and if there is nothing to build on, you can not do business, and if you can not do business, we might as well shut this operation down.

Stabbing D would be messy. And he'd be much more likely to get caught. All that physical evidence like on TV.

I hope you'll take this to heart, D said.

I'll certainly try, he said.

D flinched. What does that mean?

I'll take it to heart.

What did you mean *try?*

I didn't mean anything.

No?

No.

D stared at him. I hope not.

He could garrote D. That might be the best way. Or poison.

He was thinking of poison as D shut the door behind him.

Driver

Some said he never was a doctor. My brother, now this was my own brother, claimed one October to have seen him driving a truck—a flatbed, I believe it was, with wooden cattle corralling around the bed—a truck filled with ripe orange pumpkins.

I do not see how such a thing could have happened. How, for that matter, my brother could have been sure. A truck passes, you look at the driver, see him for an instant and believe him to be an acquaintance. Surely everyone has had this experience.

Most, of course, admit their mistakes to themselves. This was not the style of our family, and over the years, my brother's assertion became, if anything, more forceful.

—In a truck, he would say, filled to the gunwales with pumpkins.

—To the what? I would say.

—To the hilt? I would say.

My brother would pound the table or break a bottle, threaten some type of violence.

I would beg off.

By then, what was it to me?

I had never known Doctor to drive anything, nor had I known him to garden, farm, or procreate. He lived in a brick house. The brick was red once, but the sun had faded it to more of a mud color. People, usually people in the trades, would ask about the brick, mention the possibilities. I don't know what the possibilities were. Sandblasting—it seems that certainly sandblasting would have been an option. Or paint, maybe.

Doctor was not interested in the possibilities.

He would ask about dogs.

Doctor burnt a growth off my body with a tool that reminded me of a soldering iron. The smell—burning flesh, I supposed—was sickening and the smoke rising from me and the implement was bluish.

—What type of dog is best for squirrels? Doctor said.

I thought it was a joke. I said I didn't know, and I waited.

—What about deer? Elk? Use the same type of dog for deer and elk, or do you need two different breeds?

I shrugged.

—And bear? Doctor said. Hell of a dog that goes for bear.

—I don't hunt, I said.

Doctor nodded. —I see. You're the type of boy that likes to stay home, is that it? You can tell me; I am a licensed physician.

—That's not what I meant, I said.

—I put it wrong, Doctor said. I meant, what kind of watchdog do you have?

—Well, I said.

—Big or small? Bark or bite? Something that scares strangers off? What's the meanest, the most ferocious, the best breed in property protection?

I never saw a dog in his yard. Most of the yard was surrounded by a high, ragged hedge. The hedge grew over and out of a rotting wood and wire fence, but the fence was only waist high at best, in the spots where it didn't sag, and the hedge was a good seven feet.

At that time I did not know that there were two kinds of brick houses, good and bad. How could I have known?

It was my aspiration, my hope and dream and mission, to get the hell out of that town, that house, that life. My brother could not seem to understand me. No one seemed to. However, it took money. I found a little job unloading trucks and saved every penny. One day, my back went out. I could not stand up straight; I was frozen half-bent, twisted.

It was over to his office. The office was at the front of the house; it looked like it might have been a porch or verandah at one time and then rebuilt and subdivided into three or four tiny exam cubicles.

Doctor forced me down on my stomach on the exam table. It hurt. My face stuck to the paper covering.

—Yow, I said.

—Shut up, Doctor said. He was feeling along my spine. —You strained it. Cramps, don't it? Pulled it this way and that, a big strong-looking boy like you.

—Cement, I said. We had a truck load of it over at the lumber yard.

—Saw a car down by the river looked like your dad's, Doctor said. Last night. Something going on there—smooch, smooch, smooch. Who's your little pal?

—It wasn't me, I said.

—A double? Pretty cramped in there for a rangy boy like you. Easy to pull your back.

He jammed his finger between my vertebrae. —I knew a man once who was married to a cat.

I screamed.

—Soon, Doctor said, they'll fix everything with robot machines.

My brother got out before me without a thought, without a wish, and came back and picked up his life, along with a considerable amount of money. How he got it, I never understood. He explained it to me many times as though it were the simplest thing in the world, but I seemed to have always missed something. Me, I got out too, eventually, for about fifteen years but landed back as broke and confused and stupid as I'd been as a kid. I managed to get an apartment over a storefront and my brother got me a little job with the state.

I never saw Doctor around, and after awhile, I asked what ever became of him.

—He's still in his house, my brother said.

I drove by the place—just the same, only fifteen years worse. The hedge twelve feet high. There was a sign on the gate, that was new. It listed hours, ten a week; clearly he was semi-retired.

I didn't know how old he was.

I remembered him as—well—not young or old. Eternally middle-aged, maybe.

I wanted a bit of healing, so for old time's sake, I went to see him. The office was the same except the old woman who had worked as a receptionist was gone. She was replaced by a sign, black magic marker on cardboard, that said GO IN. The arrow pointed to one of the cubicles.

I loosened my tie and sat on the exam table.

My brother told me he had once seen Doctor in a boat give himself an injection of morphine. My brother could not persuasively explain how he knew that it was morphine, or when this had happened, or what he, my brother, was doing there in the boat with Doctor.

Doctor was smoking a cigarette, a straight, when he came into the exam room.

I explained the nature of my complaint.

He nodded, flicked the ash into a white plastic ashtray with the name of a popular birth control pill on it, took my blood pressure. He thumped my chest, checked my pulse, peered into my eyes, felt my liver.

I could not tell if he remembered me; he looked into my ears and nostrils with his little pen light.

—This, Doctor said, is the way it's going to happen. A little spot, a little blemish, a little something you'll notice, and that's it. For some sooner, more dramatically. I'll take my time. I'll wait.

I asked if it was okay for me to put my shoes back on.

—That's the beauty of it, Doctor said. At the end they let you out; you go free of everything.

He handed me a prescription.

—Knew a man once, he said, couldn't go on. We left him with a pistol and told him he'd have to do a certain little thing for us.

I buttoned up my shirt.

—You see these movies they make now? Doctor said.

I asked my brother what had happened, but it did not add up.

—He caught a chill, my brother said, that never went away. It was worse than we thought. He'd been out there, first time we saw him much in years, after deer season, making people take pictures of him with his gun.

—After that, my brother shook his head.

It wasn't, I guess, nothing to me, but it wasn't much to me either.

Then my brother started in about the truck and the pumpkins. Only this time, it was Christmas day and Jesus Christ was driving and the bed was full of bushels of corn.

Suits

I am a man who wears three coats, although I only wear all three at the same time when it's really cold. I have a hooded sweatshirt, a vest filled with some insulating material, and a shapeless cotton shell called, I believe, a chore coat. A chore coat they call it, as though I were a farmer, as though I spent a part of my day, say afternoon or early morning, doing chores.

I sell things over the telephone for a job.

I don't know what that makes me. A salesman maybe. Maybe not.

I was waiting outside the revival movie theater. My brother and sister were inside, delayed by some acquaintance of theirs. No friend of mine, that fellow.

When they came out, we went to the coffee shop in my brother's car. My brother did not see how the movie was supposed to be so great.

My sister thought the movie was sad.

Okay, we had seen the movie, okay, it was about poor people, and okay, it was sad. But those suits, I said, and remember this was half a world away. Or a quarter world. You know, like a quadrant or whatever the people who know call it.

My sister was explaining what cafe latte was. She had taken to doing this over the last ten years or so, and frankly it was beginning to annoy me.

My brother unzipped his parka. He wore a T-shirt from one cigarette company and a baseball cap from another. I noticed a duffle bag from yet another company in his car.

My sister ordered ordinary coffee and poured skim milk into it until it was the color of an earthworm. My brother had some sweet foreign drink made from a viscous syrup.

They do this because they know I'm sensitive.

I noticed my brother's watch had the logo of a popular menthol on it.

Maybe I'll go downtown next week, I said, and get me one of those suits.

Not that I could not have had a better coat, a single coat instead of the three. I had some extra money, a bonus in fact, from selling a lot of things over the phone. I could have had a down-filled parka like my brother's, identical, had I wanted to. I knew where he'd bought his, what he paid, what comparable brands were going for.

But it seemed they did not make the coat I wanted. All the coats in the world, and I could not find the kind I like.

Not that I gave it much thought, with everything at work. At work, there was a new thing. There was the team concept: We were all a team working towards the same thing, a win. We were all important. What we said, what we thought about how we could win, was important. We had to respect each other and each other's ideas.

I was not more important than you, for example.

Some pom poms were fastened to the bulletin board, for example.

I had forgotten all about suits, and I was putting in extra hours at work, so I did not see movies with my siblings very often. I ran into my brother at a supermarket on a Sunday morning. I had gone in early to get some juice and the paper.

My brother was holding a carton of cigarettes. A free deck of cards was attached to the carton. He asked me did I remember this guy we had gone to school with.

Of course, I said. Certainly I remembered this guy.

This guy, my brother said, was dead. He had been doing some roofing work when he was struck by lightning.

I remembered this guy like it was yesterday. Remembered how he had looked then. I hadn't seen him in years; we all looked different now. I certainly looked different now.

The orange juice carton felt slippery in my hand.

We don't, any of us, do things the way they used to. For example, I don't throw dirt in a grave. I don't go to the grave, for that matter, if I can avoid it. Or to the church. The prayers and the priest, they were nothing to me anymore. It was hard to believe they were ever anything to anybody, they seemed so small, so old.

Other things you have to do, and I needed a suit. I looked. My sister gave me a ride. She went through the stores, the good stores, feeling coat sleeves and saying, this is good, or try this one. There was nothing for me. Anything any good was way too high.

Thanks for the lift, I told her. I knew she was annoyed. I knew what she thought about me.

I had to check the sales flyers, the discount houses. Nobody paid full price now. My sister had come in for coffee. She was sorting through the paper, and she handed me a flyer. Look, she said.

There it was. Separates. You got the pants and the coat off the rack, low price, no alterations. They looked okay. Not great, not the suits in the movies, but within the realm of acceptability.

On sale now, the basic navy model featured in the fuzzy picture. And there were smaller pictures, pictures almost as small as my thumbnail, of striped and patterned suits.

I squinted a little, trying to bring them into focus. I noticed it said *fancy suits*. The price on these *fancy suits* was ten dollars higher than the price on the basic suits.

Fancy suits, I said, are we going back in time? Is this grandpa's day?

Gonna go to town and get myself a fancy suit.

The clerk wanted to know if I needed an overcoat.

I had a better idea on that one.

The clerk put a plastic bag over the suit and hanger.

My sister drove me to the Veteran's Thrift Store. Good selection, but the overcoats were all tan. I had hoped to get a black one.

Tan would be okay. Cleaned and Pressed, tan would be fine.

At the end, my brother came over to me and whispered the name of the bar where everyone was going. He whispered, whispered almost sweetly, in my ear.

Okay, I said.

I walked into that dark bar, in the one room, and I knew everyone would be in the back room. Funny what I thought. I'd been in that bar many times, a million times before, but never in a suit.

It all seemed a little unreal.

My brother had told me the widow and the two little kids—I hadn't even known this guy was married—would get some money, some settlement.

I thought about something I'd read when I left school. I'd read that the best investment for a new grad was a good quality blue suit. I remembered my father saying the best investment was a percentage of income set aside monthly in mutual funds.

I was walking to the back room, and I remembered my mother reading me a story, a story about a guy who got a new coat and how it changed his life.

Architecture of the French Novel

Sunday afternoon in September, rain and the wood piled in the yard black in the rain. Not far, in the center of the city, were several well-known pieces of public art, so many and so well known, the city was sometimes known as the City of Public Art although he was not persuaded the sobriquet was not the result of a civic campaign rather than spontaneous coinage. The statues were, no doubt, as wet as the wood and stood in the rain like other statuary—well known relics of civilizations that remained after the belief which had engendered them.

He thought years before life had a more industrial quality. The then industrial quality of life he remembered. After all, he had worked then—he'd been very young—for an industrial concern. A truck would come around, and from the driver one could buy cigarettes, sandwiches, soft drinks. The Mobile Chef. He wondered if mobile chef trucks any longer existed. It was difficult to know what to call such a truck; eventually he came up with canteen truck. Surely no one used such a phrase today—that language had vanished with the trucks and that more industrial quality of life and why would he feel even the slightest nostalgia for it.

Because he had been there.

Because he had been young.

Dead, the past.

Like the dead man.

The dead man deader in the past as the past lived on in his memory.

As did the dead man.

While he was at the industrial concern, the dead man had worked at a store. He remembered going into the store and seeing the dead man—both youths then—the dead man was wearing an apron and bagging groceries. The store cleaner, easier work than the industrial concern. He suspected the store paid better than the industrial concern. The work at the industrial concern dirty and dangerous.

In a sense that visit to the store his introduction to commerce. He wondered that day if the dead man were not more intelligent than he.

On this rainy Sunday nothing on television but a cheap movie.

Zombie movie.

He'd seen it many years before on the late night horror show.

Heard the dead man was found in a lake. Later, heard it was a pond. He imagined the rain falling in the pond as the body floated there.

Another version the dead man found hanging.

Rope.

Red dart through the trees. Cardinal. A bird named for a medieval European concept.

A bird an allusion.

The wet leaves. The sexual texture of the world.

Two murders in that morning's paper. One had done it for love. The other for hatred. Because I hated everything the comment.

The dead man had hated everything though at first it seemed the dead man had only hated everything at the end. Then he realized the dead man had hated everything from the beginning.

The unburied. Of course the dead man was buried. Or cremated.

Cremated quickly in shame.

Abandoned. As the dead man had, in a sense, abandoned everyone.

The one who did it for love said for me it was all an accident, something I could not prevent.

He'd had the feeling the dead man would kill himself. If not that, the feeling of something else.

When they were young, he wore a second-hand coat of heavy wool in the winter. He'd once slept on the dead man's floor and had that coat for a blanket, he remembered. That was how it was in those times. They'd do anything as though they thought it were nothing.

He thought of the dead man's wife. Every myth a family drama. Her name was Penelope. Odd. Penelope the dead man's wife her name now. If she were still alive he did not know. Dead Penelope the dead man's wife if not. All of it too cumbersome. When he had broken with the dead man the final time, he vowed he would never utter the dead man's name again. The dead man, he thought, was at that time dead to him. But it was too cumbersome. He had to rename the dead man.

Renaming the dead man a complicated thing. He ran through a number of names but they all were associated with other people—friends, relatives, coworkers. He did not want the dead man to carry an association with the living.

He decided on *Jules*.

Jules' wife, he thought of her.

Silence but for the falling rain. As though one could step forever out of any entanglement.

No myth of what was not completed. No myth of incompleteness. Were the myths myths of capability?

Alive once.

Birds named for medieval concepts.

Dead men.

Jules' wife portrayed herself as something of an innocent, as though things were always surprising and new to her. He did not know if he'd liked this or hated this. At best it could be refreshing; at worst it implied an idiotic enthusiasm. He never mentioned it to Jules, for it would certainly have been inappropriate to have done so. He'd felt sure she was evaluating him. He'd felt beneath her innocence she was trying to see what if anything he was worth.

Some calculation behind her eyes.

A sexual tension perhaps.

Jules and Penelope. Penelope and Jules.

Jules never fully trusted him. He never fully trusted Penelope.

Jules never fully trusted him though they had hunted together in the snow as brothers might if brothers were as friends and not at bitter war.

Jules had a place at a lake. Inherited. Land in his family for years. He'd had no land in the family nor inheritance. Whatever had once been was lost years before he was born.

Not that it mattered.

Not that he missed it.

He was not much of a hunter though Jules was quite good and as good hunted only occasionally. Jules was not much for hunting, Jules said.

All of this years, years ago. He and Penelope and Jules.

Who buries the dead?

When does Jules get buried for good?

For once.

Certainly something was done with the corpse. It's not as if they'd leave the corpse sitting at the dining room table. But it seemed no one had taken care of it.

In the water.

Or hanging in a tree.

He'd thought at the time of the death, Penelope would have called him. And then? He would have comforted her, he felt, to the extent he would have been able to comfort anyone.

Never heard from her. He'd broken with Jules years before. Perhaps he'd broken with her by extension. Or she was dead. Or she'd left Jules and begun a new life or she simply did not wish to communicate with him.

He imagined her in some other life without Jules now. A trim, organized, middle-aged woman she'd be. A woman who held herself together by accepting the limitations in her life, who relentlessly controlled her life through limitation. There had always been something grimly pragmatic about Penelope.

Her casual acceptance of sexual need.

Standing at the window. Observing the houses across the cul-de-sac out of what visual obsession. The rain heavy enough to be visible in the air.

How long would he stand there, he thought. How long had he ever stood there? On one occasion, not in total. He did not know. No reason for him to know.

He contemplated the past as metaphor. The future as metaphor. None was apt. Not to anything. The practice of metaphor, perhaps, wrong.

At least in this context.

Hadn't he heard all this many years ago in a course he had taken called *The Elements of Drama?*

The future, he understood, would be comprised of moments. Everything would be of the moment and the past would inevitably disappear in the future's temporal discontinuity.

He would try—as he presumed would others—to cling to his life as an insect clings to the outside of a jar of honey.

Sometimes he felt Jules—the dead Jules—would pull him under as Jules had pulled himself under.

If he had—

If there were any possibility of *if* to it.

It was not a feeling. There was no depth of feeling, but a vacuum as though vacuums developed like whirlpools one from the next.

Only last week, he had been mistaken in the street for someone he did not know.

Disappointment in the woman's eyes.

It seemed the slow downward spiral of identity. But that could not have been so. He disappeared from her eyes when he was not who she expected. The disappearance final.

That sense of life diverted. That sensation of past action, of passing time.

Jules had never lived in some greasy suburb. He never faced—he never made his living in the culture of the swapmeet. So much was spared him yet he was, of all things, dead.

If it weren't raining today, there would be a sale somewhere in the cul-de-sac. Only so much clement weather, and one had to use it as one could.

Penelope might make it at a swapmeet. She seemed more able to accept things.

Not that she had been entirely successful in the theater of love. With Jules, how could she have been?

That constructed monster.

That monster who built himself as a monster.

The advantage of the swapmeet the clarity of purchase. Everything subject to open examination and appraisal. Haggling, if not encouraged, allowed. He had often bought things—food—that had pictures of their contents on the packages. What was inside did not look like the picture. Even then, he would go back and buy the same things. He could not separate what he wanted from it from what annoyed him in it. There was an inevitability to this. What was the word for that?

Was there a word for that?

Penelope had in a way been always appraising him. He did not know it at the time. He only realized it after he became aware of Jules' death.

Which was after the fact.

As was so much in life, though the world went forward.

When he was a child, there was a painting in the hallway of his grade school, a Gaugin of a woman with a mango. He believed the painting was called *Woman with a Mango*.

At that time, in that part of the world, there were no mangos. The teachers explained a mango was some kind of tropical fruit.

Now he could buy them in any store. Now he could buy many things that had not existed then. Yet knowing that, remembering that, he had no idea when he had first tasted a mango or when that once absent fruit had ceased to be exotic.

But what fruit could matter on a rainy Sunday in a suburb?

With dead Jules in mind.

If there had been distance between them, they had created it.

Certainly they had once been close.

Now their fallings out, their senseless quarrels, seemed as spare as a minimalist play. Some stark drama. Surely it had been a busier picture—all active fore- and background—as he lived it.

For Jules as well though it was ridiculous to speculate upon what Jules may or may not have perceived. At times it seemed as though Jules manipulated every turn in their relationship, but at other times he was equally aware of feeling Jules was incapable of conceiving, much less manipulating, anything.

That argument almost within a family, meaningless like some old myth. Those betrayals long and slow and sudden and quick.

He and Jules would go to the village near Jules' cabin and drink in a small, wood-paneled bar with the other cabin people and the locals. A sense of being away from the city, of some rustic pleasure. The drinking, the fishing, the hunting, the woods, the lake. Why was he condemned to work backwards and forwards through his life? Remembering those frosty mugs and later estrangements. The arguments based in misunderstandings still not clearly understood.

Friends fall away, naturally.

Isolation, natural.

Death, of course, follows.

A matter of pattern. Common, inevitable pattern.

Maybe there was a theater of love but there was no auditorium of love.

Or if there were, the auditorium of love was not the theater of love. The dreams enacted within made all the difference.

Did Penelope know Jules would destroy himself and, if so, did she slyly encourage him in that destruction? And how could she do that? By going along with him. By letting him do what he wanted while knowing what it would cost him. By whispering her suspicions of everyone and every thing in his ear.

Did Jules do the same to her? Was it a race, a folie a deux, something mutual, reciprocal, based inside their marriage?

Was that mutually-encouraged self destruction their love?

If she was destroyed.

Jules would have had him believe Jules contemplated the fundamental questions of meaning, of life. Of course, Jules had mentioned those questions but that mention a gesture of emotional need, not thought.

Jules could not think; he was certain of that.

Whether Penelope could think remained unresolved.

Jules mistook his constant self regard, the constant reflection of Jules' needs, for thought as though even if Jules had been able to think, thought could not have led Jules to anything. The man too inherently flawed for that.

His flaw perhaps the reason he was unable to think. Though Penelope certainly had her flaws. and she could, possibly, think, but there was no clear evidence of that.

Yet what had marked Jules when he first met Jules more than anything was Jules' charm. His wit. His generosity. His kindness. Jules seemed one of the most charming people he had ever met. Jules helped him with small things—rides—he did not at that time drive—cigarettes, money. He was penniless all those years ago and Jules thought nothing of lending a hundred or two hundred dollars. Interest free.

Jules sympathized with him.

Jules was sympathetic.

Jules assured him Jules understood that no one understood him. This was in advance of Penelope.

Not that Penelope was to blame for Jules' later behavior.

Not that Jules' later behavior was in opposition to Jules' earlier behavior.

He knew now, though he did not understand at the time, Jules' earlier behavior was merely a set up for Jules' later behavior.

Cunningly so.

That a man could understand the arc of his behavior over years, set it up and see its fruition, was cunning.

Brilliantly so.

It took him years to see it. Because he never planned his behavior. Because there was neither arc nor fruition to his behavior. Because he was blind to any subtly, to every guile. Because he was a fool.

As a fool, the perfect victim of a person like Jules.

It was not that simple.

Nothing could be that simple. In this world.

Jules had made a victim of him, but, he suspected, he had made a victim of Jules. Or Jules had made a victim of himself.

In a tree.

In a lake.

He'd told a story about Jules that was not strictly true. He changed what Jules had said to make the story better. While he was doing it, he knew he was doing it, but he did not think about doing it. Not then. Later. Later he thought he should not have altered the story.

He realized only he and Jules knew what Jules had actually said and Jules was dead.

Only he knew.

The story belonged to him.

Dead, Jules belonged to whoever might make use of him.

How the wind howled out here when it stormed.

How the rain carried in sheets on that wind.

Even the Jules of the story, the improved Jules, was at the time of the story developing his obstructionist stance of the future.

The family exacted its revenge. Jules got a cremation quick and quiet. Gone before anyone knew it. Before any published notice. Up the stack and out the air. Cremation once forbidden. Erasure. Erased, why would Jules refuse so vehemently to disappear?

Ideas popping like rockets in his head as rain washed the suburb.

He'd been manipulated every step of the way. Someone told him. Framed as a narrative, it might look that way.

His wife had said it.

One night at the table.

She had set him a place with a plate he would not eat off. The plate unappetizing—sickening—in its color and design. He told her he would not use it and that was what she said.

Wasn't it.

2

Some mornings, he took a complicated network of streets and arteries which took him past a series of woods and lakes.

It was as though he were driving through the woods though he was not.

The wooded areas and big houses overlooking the lakes belonged to the privileged.

The lakes were not his privilege but were beautiful in the morning light—gray or sun. Looking at them a pleasure, it seemed, that grew with age. Though he'd enjoyed his time, mostly, at Jules' lake place.

Up there once, he remembered, with a woman so clean and crisp in herself he liked to watch her in the slightest act. He had watched her as she ate a melon.

Eat the melon, he said.

Or she said it.

That much was clear. Beyond that his memory of her somewhat obscure. The fundamental questions could not be asked and so were not asked. He remembered that.

As to what those questions were, hardly meaningful to consider. No more to be asked now than then. Fundamental as they were, to ask them, then and now, irrelevant.

That woman had said this was all about love.

He did not understand exactly what she meant.

She said she was a nurse and she'd seen many people die and all of them had died happy because they were going home.

Clearly she was insane.

Jules had introduced her to him. Had Jules done it as a joke, knowing she was crazy, or had Jules done it as malice, to humiliate him, or could it have been possible Jules had introduced her innocently, unaware she was crazy?

They had eaten out doors beneath a canopy at a folding table.

Shaded, they ate in a shady breeze.

The fact that she was crazy, crazy with the ridiculous beliefs of the world they—he and Jules—had come from, or he, at least, for with Jules one could never be absolutely sure. If he'd come from some other world none of this would have mattered, but though he was leaving the world he'd come from, he could not destroy, could not eradicate, that world. Not in fact. Not within himself.

Yet she was so beautiful.

This, in some reckoning, should have told him who he was.

Who he was?

Even now, he thought he would drive out to Jules' cabin but knew there was nothing there. Nothing but lake and forest, which was, in its totality, nothing enough.

Jules had said, this is made of that. That is made of this. One tries to see the difference. A dog. A cat. A rat. You. Me.

At the time he believed Jules was talking nonsense. Mocking him. Now he knew Jules was lying.

His wife had said he had talked all the time about what was essential.

What was essential?

He did not remember anything like that.

Not at all.

Of course, he'd been a fool.

If that was her point.

And why had he thought of visiting Jules' wrecked homestead when he knew he was awaiting a wreck of his own? No place was going to tell him anything. A place told nothing.

There was nothing to tell.

He knew what had happened.

Not to Jules.

Not the details.

Details did not matter. Details, which always seemed so important at the time, never mattered whatsoever.

Jules and those *If I Don't Survive the Night* cards, those annoying cards that made Jules a fortune on top of the money already left Jules. Every fantastic creation out Jules' mouth turning a profit. The birth of the gods, almost. The gods dollars or accumulations of dollars or representation of dollars.

Do you envy him? Penelope had asked him. It never occurred to him until the moment of her utterance he might envy Jules. He did not remember what he told her.

Something noncommittal he was certain.

All that talk from Jules about horses, about how Jules would put up a stable and riding ring at the cabin and get some horses. It was not clear to him what Jules was pretending to. The gentry? The west? Some imaginary combination of the two?

He, if he were the richest man in the world, would never own a horse.

Yet Jules was the type who just might. That was what allowed Jules to make such reckless and nonsensical assertions.

Was he supposed to miss Jules?

He did not know if he missed Jules or not. Or which Jules, friend or enemy? Sometimes easier to miss an enemy than a friend. At times one wanted friends to disappear. As he was often sick of himself, he was often sick of his friends, of the continuity of life.

Jules had wanted it over, and for Jules it was over now.

He could understand how Jules felt though he could not understand why Jules felt that way. And Penelope. It seemed Penelope had done nothing to assist Jules.

To comfort him.

Penelope not the type to bring comfort. Something too sharp and feral in her intelligence for that.

In her understanding of the world.

Her lack of illusion. Or sympathy. Or comfort. Jules had willed her upon himself. If anything was surprising, it was that Penelope was willing to go along with Jules.

One used to say, to share his life.

Now she was not sharing Jules' life and she obviously had not been sharing it for some time.

Unless he was wrong.

He did not know that she was not there, that she, as he suspected, left to lead a life of her own long before Jules went into the water.

Or up into the tree.

He could not have done both.

Could he?

One after the next? Succeeding in one after he'd failed in the other. If Penelope were not there, how quiet the woods when Jules had finished. Completely done. Alone there with no one watching. Jules at that point in a sense a part of the forest. Element in the landscape. Or the water.

Jules, then, belonged to nothing and no one.

He had to remind himself he too belonged to no one. Jules reminded him—the thought of Jules reminded him to remind himself. He had to do this occasionally for he sometimes had the sense he belonged to something. He would not willingly be the prisoner of a construct. Not now. It might be a mistake he'd made or would make in another venue.

Jules steely as a snake. Scaly as a snake. His skin condition.

Even Jules had his complaints. But they were further obfuscations in the form of clarity. The language neatly manufactured, the instruments of measurement precisely invoked.

I understand the point of confusion, Jules said. Jules said that all the time.

The phrases that seemed initial eloquence were obviously automatically generated. He wondered if Jules had been truly conscious. Sometimes he suspected Penelope was with Jules to observe Jules as though she were studying a reptile on a Pacific Island. It could have been that way from the start. Or perhaps some of Jules' poison spilled into her and blossomed like the black flower of cancer in his imagination.

He knew the dream of a truly depraved woman and could not believe Jules would not share such a dream. Penelope seemed not to observe even the outer forms of depravity.

The double wife. Another possible affectation for Jules. Like the thread in his car, a thread from his old hunting coat which Jules said he could not throw away. The thread in his car for years.

That thread like a habit.

Nothing in his car. Maybe a map. Or a coffee mug. Nothing unnecessary. Nothing preserved or displayed or commented on for the passengers' edification.

Why hadn't Penelope thrown the thread away? She must have heard Jules' ponderous speech about it a thousand times.

And a thread. As though it were a pet or a photo. A memento. A memento of Jules' false persona. The hunter.

The hunter in retirement.

The hunter in repose.

Penelope had said it was about love.

This was supposed to be insightful. He did not understand exactly what she meant. As when Jules told that story about the rocks that were thrown and the rocks came alive and wreaked their terrible revenge. He did not know what Jules meant. Or the story. It was Jules' business to know stories and what they meant. It was not his business to know any of it.

Jules said the story was about the crisis of belief.

How could Jules characterize anything as a crisis of belief? The words meant nothing.

Nonsense, every bit of it.

How was he to feel about people he had loved and hated? Why could he not move on?

That water. The tree.

Later the omelet. Bread. Red wine. The modest supper of the alone.

He had no need to be reminded of what was lost and no desire to revisit what remained to be lost.

Sometimes he thought he heard his name spoken. This terrified him.

Perhaps Penelope and Jules had had an understanding he was not aware of.

They were that type or they were not.

He had to remember a public project was not the private project nor did the private project owe anything to the public project.

He did not know.

His wife might have known. His wife had understood no one knew anything but the suspicion someone might know something she did not know drove her mad. Their marriage, he believed, had had the fascination of a disaster at a distance. Not that he could refute her view or his belief she held that view. At the end she'd gone in all good will and he had nothing to say to her. Their formerly fundamental relations and questions of life and death—fine, but beyond that, what?

Perhaps Jules and Penelope were the same towards the end.

He had seen the purity of the impending disaster against the impure qualities of quotidian life.

Who had not?

They—he and his wife—had had a portrait in the house. The only framed item. His wife had taken it when she left or it had been lost in the sale of and move from that house. It did not matter. No art necessary in this rising suburb.

He had seen ducks—mallards—flying through the rain over his yard.

No one, he understood, believed any longer in sorrow. Nor did he. Sorrow seemed, if not ridiculous, antique, inappropriate.

When they'd had the portrait, they thought they were better than where they were from or where they lived. They saw themselves exceptional, better than their past, their present.

And the future?

Jules and all his advantage had a strong sense of himself which Jules to all his advantage concealed beneath a shell of feigned insecurity. A monster garbed in the cloak of the sensitive.

Hidden and ethereal as to be nothing, he had no sense of himself.

Jules' constant demands for reassurance, his pretense of neediness, he now realized, were an act played for everyone but Penelope. Which meant, he reasoned, Penelope had seen through Jules from the start.

Had she controlled Jules?

As Jules had attempted to control him, though Penelope, as he recalled, showed no need for reassurance from anyone. If Penelope were anything, she was certain. Certitude embodied, which seemed to him an odd quality in a woman.

He was not sure.

Jules dead, Penelope dead or gone, his wife long gone.

He had no one to talk to.

There was no one he wanted to talk to.

Even at his work he avoided conversation.

Whatever they thought they had been saying they had talked only nonsense.

Now it was the noose.

It was the water.

The pills.

Jules.

Was he secretly or not so secretly pleased or was he merely after all this indifferent?

Jules' claim that life should be the pursuit of a singular great enthusiasm as though Jules were some Victorian gentleman explorer. Even if the notion had some merit it took money and only someone with money would entertain such nonsense.

He did not think about the money in his account. Jules tracked Jules' money with computerized accounting systems. Or so Jules said. Jules was not one of those to make do though he seemed to believe others would always make do.

Build their enthusiasms—their great enthusiasms—on whatever was available to them.

Jules implied he was wasting his life.

He was.

Jules was not.

The exquisite medium of implication.

3

Nothing but bitterness.

He knew bitterness well and wore it like a coat. It seemed it inhered in Jules like Jules' blood or skeleton or lungs.

The constant unrecognized petulance.

The barely suppressed rage.

The billowing sheets of rain different here.

The dark of night darker here.

In all his pettiness, his venality, Jules still more venal than he?

When someone disappears the stories multiply.

Jules perhaps and perhaps Penelope seemed to represent some truth he could or would not face. About himself.

Or the world.

Or the three of them.

What did it matter if he'd desired Penelope? They were all young then. And it was not so much desire as knowledge of—acknowledgement of—possibility.

Before his wife.

Penelope's hand in the small of his back an oddly intimate gesture as though it had been burned there.

He seemed empty now; he'd seemed empty before. Always. From his first consciousness.

And nothing happened.

And he did not do anything.

Penelope wore a sweater heavy and soft that draped her so.

The day black and white as tundra in winter. Gray and off-white as the long waning day.

This was in the snow you realize.

Leave it to Jules to wait to sodden fall and put a tree into it. The water too baptismal for him and the tree structural, approximating a sculpture— the necessary—inevitable—grandiosity.

Maybe they sheltered you as long as they could as they might a child, his wife had said.

As they might? he'd said.

No one had sheltered him from anything. She knew that.

He had to remind himself he belonged to no one and nothing.

His wife had betrayed him with no regret. It was something that happened, she said.

Jules she told him had tried to seduce her.

But she had not betrayed him with Jules.

She had betrayed him with someone else.

Where he had come from betrayal was treated with cautious ignorance or immediate violence.

He simply told his wife it was time for her to go and she agreed. She seemed surprised as he was she had not gone already.

The idea that anything could rise above itself. That they might rise above themselves.

They did not.

Why should betrayal mean anything at all?

Why should a fact be more than a fact.

The unbearable past layered on the unbearable yet strangely quiet present.

Too much for Jules.

Jules felled as it were.

Jules and the film that was not.

Jules and the building that was not.

Jules and the future that was not.

Maybe he had hated himself but he had not hated himself as much as Jules had hated him. He had not hated himself even as much as Jules had hated himself. Certainly he did not hate himself to the point he would behave as Jules had behaved.

Leave all this, his wife said.

He had not understood.

He had sometimes thought he was perhaps mentally ill.

Not severely.

Mildly.

He had looked up one day to see Jules on television in enraged commentary.

He had heard that Jules once wore a cape on an airplane. A cape—in that strange somnambulance of air travel.

Jules had been other than he remembered Jules being.

The question of what was under this what was foundational to this as though something were under this as though the notion that anything were under anything had any longer any purchase.

Had Penelope said that?

Penelope, he'd heard, burned the cabin. Unless it was Jules. Or lightning.
Her animal appeal undoubted.

That beautiful cabin.

To possess the object of beauty what did that mean did that mean anything how could anything mean nothing or was it the other way.

People wanted beautiful things.

Nonsense. Penelope said that.

He did not recall what Jules responded.

The cabin the water the tree the woods.

Why would this goddamned forest give up no respite. Why must it eternally prosecute itself. Dead to all the past why should he care.

There was nothing.

Jules knew what he could do. What he could do for Jules. What he could do for Jules was what he must do as far as Jules was concerned. And done.

Done.

A belief in thought or feeling which seemed a kind of thought one might as well lecture in geometry.

As though some suspended sexual intrigue some suspended jeopardy meant anything. Penelope well aware of the distance between people. Of silence. Absence.

If you're going to drink Jules said drink without mercy.

Penelope gorgeous. And rich.

He did not need to remind himself.

There was nothing to keep anyone from trying to get to her.

Jules obsessively created internalized rules obsessively—games really—in deliberate obstinate ignorance of the world as it was. He wondered if Jules carried this habit into Jules' sexual activities with Penelope.

Jules claimed watching the history of Japan on television caused Jules to burst into tears.

Why would not Jules' tears be as nonsensical as all Jules' other games? Jules was after all a pretender to a kind of purity.

What purity did you have in mind, his wife said. He was not sure what they had been talking about but quite possibly they had been talking about Jules.

And Penelope.

A beautiful day the day Jules died. Beauty of the day chilled him. He thought about all the beautiful days after him. No story, only a collection of facts.

Jules claimed to have once lived on Winter Street. Nonsense. As Jules claim Jules descended from an obscure subgallic regal figure, The King With Three Crowns.

Jules closed up now like a cabinet of curios.

Sealed in.

Burned up first to be fair.

Royalty. Jules who wore the windbreaker of a discount airline.

Logo.

He had a carry-on with a logo on it. The logo of his former organization. That he had once been a member of an organization incredible.

In Jules' defense Jules compared to the doleful plump businessmen of the region seemed pure energy.

Though Jules, after all, utter mediocrity.

Done, Jules was.

And he not quite done.

That the measurement, the irresistible measuring.

One could not stop from it if one wanted to and he did not want to.

Why should he?

Jules believed there was a way to lead life without mercy.

He hoped for mercy. Wrongfully and wrong-headedly.

He sometimes wondered whether Jules lived truly in this world at all.

This world the world he lived in. He was not one to speak about the leaden quality of everything.

Penelope strong, self-assured, able, seemingly, to face anything.

Failure.

Jules' failure the money gone. Jules had tried to cheat him out of what little money he had. That and the attempted seduction of his wife. And Jules putting it about to their circle that he had no ideas that any and all of his ideas were truly Jules' ideas. Yet when Jules failed, who could Jules turn to to say how Jules had been destroyed? Jules unable to sincerely beg his forgiveness or to send Penelope to attempt to broker a reconciliation.

Could the situation have been reversed? He had never failed as Jules did but he had less to lose and was unable to overextend himself as Jules had.

He would never have reconnected with Jules under any circumstance. He was certain of that.

The business, the empire of nothing. Like a store that sold nothing. All gone. Vanished.

No business for him. He was unable to master the rudiments of the art. Jules' belief in control.

Jules ridiculous claim that as a child Jules had lived on L'Entendre Street.

As though he were on Understanding Avenue in this sodden suburb.

I'll be purely for you in the moment. Jules had said that. He had no understanding of whether Jules was attempting to express anything.

As when Jules discussed the film Jules planned to make.

A story in pictures. The notion old—ancient—yet recurring. Here again as these things unfortunately tend to be.

How one might fall and catch.

How one might drown.

The tree, the water. One might go here, there. Any where. No everything to it. No sum.

No something to it.

If Jules had not seen all that years ago clearly Jules had seen nothing. The black wet days of those summers. Those years in the wet.

Jules speaking then of the precision of the alignments. Or was it the arrangements.

Who had he thought he was.

Who had they thought they were speaking those words now empty as ash.

He'd heard Jules had left some small paintings or drawings on cardboard. The artifacts he supposed illustrative of Jules' greatness after Jules was gone. Who else would assert his ego from the water or the tree or the ash or the monument.

Others had. Kings and so forth. Jules no doubt ascribed himself to their company.

With cardboard and ink.

Nonsense.

The rain brought the water down and the wind brought the water up even in this turgid suburb though here it was hard to remember there had been years without rain.

He was waiting.

Jules was not.

Penelope might have been. If she was she knew what she was waiting for.

He did not.

His wife had said everything was personal. She insisted there was no backdrop. He had pointed out there were converging factors that could be understood as though lined out on a map.

A complicated thing to explain.

He noticed she was not listening.

Jules had had some young people out at his place. The young people admired Jules. They listened to Jules. They, apparently, aspired to be like Jules.

He'd heard some of them wrote down things Jules said.

Those—disciples—how many—wasn't that what they were supposed to do?

He'd rather have no one listen.

A map, he'd said, was a picture, a representation. A graph of a place. An idea of a terrain. One trusted the accuracy. Impossibly impractical to verify.

The story against him solely Jules' invention to cover Jules' greed, Jules' lust. Jules' attempt to destroy him.

And he blindly believed Jules to be his friend.

The acquisitions of his lifetime the habit of the acquisition of habit. Habitually he had trusted Jules. His unfaithful wife saw Jules as the untrustworthy bastard Jules was.

She understood he supposed the transitory nature of love.

She knew the theater of love was not a variant of the auditorium of love.

Temporary.

Why would a feeling be more permanent than anything else. Stones wore to nothing.

In the rain.

Or current.

Water did it he knew. Did and undid everything.

Here it rained beyond what he could describe. Rained not as it should have rained here; rained as it should have rained somewhere else, say, Cochin China.

As though they were lost. Forced to wander in, circumnavigate, a jungle.

He had been to a jungle. Jules he suspected had not. Just at the edge he had been. He knew better than to push in.

Jules would speak for hours about varied and exemplary mechanical toys no longer available. He'd thought the toys one of Jules' interests but now he was not certain they were not one of Jules' affectations.

It had occurred to him life might proceed like an intricately geared mechanism.

Certainly it had not.

Whatever had been spoken had disappeared.

He understood that.

Now the written faded and vanished.

It could not matter.

He did not remember what he had felt. How what he'd felt had felt. Whatever it was it seemed it had mattered at the time though it meant nothing.

That was a contradiction.

Or that was not.

That was the way things were.

He could not remember if the way things were could be a contradiction.

The past reminded him of the fire balloons they'd made from newspaper and toothpicks as children. Alight, they'd rise briefly and float in elegant burning to block greasy ash.

To end in this place.

Nothing he could do about it. Some started over. Enough to have started once. Should he keep restarting? Restart at 80 if he lived to be 80? Seen some do it and seeing it filled him with disgust.

The lovers, united, depart into their world.

He had believed his wife to be charmingly eccentric then he believed her to be neurotic then he believed her to be psychotic. It seemed a natural progression.

He had not asked what she believed about him nor had he listened if she attempted to tell him.

Perhaps she thought Jules had made him a fool.

Jules who behaved as though Jules never suffered the idiotic daily chores and senseless errors that waste life.

He left awaiting an absent winter in this endless rain.

Each day it dying away from him it seemed though he each day dying away from it more likely.

No conclusion to be drawn. Though he'd lost contact with Penelope and there was no longer the possibility of contact with Jules it was as if he expected something he had not fully considered. What half-forced reconsideration buried in his head?

Everything that had been everything was nothing now. This made for some sensible thing maybe.

The surface of things all of things he believed. Played the same movie every night and drank the same vodka.

The vodka from Sweden.

Jules had spoken constantly of film.

People wanted to be happy. Either Jules understood that and used it against everyone or Jules had no understanding of it at all.

And Penelope?

Jules told him he was complicating things—that life had no complexity.

Jules told him money could be made in the manufacture of images. He could not understand it. He remembered the billiard hall, the police supply store, the army surplus store—all from childhood—and wondered what had become of the tough guys who'd done this and done that.

Creation of memory.

There is nothing as disposable as a human being. This is a fact. He tried to remember it.

He thought he was going blind in this wet suburb. There would be no
monastery or hospital, no monks or nuns to take care of him. Such places
no longer existed—products of an outdated social model.

Suicide, maybe, Jules had said.

As though he should live in a haunted palace of forgiveness.

Blind he would remain unforgiving.

He was never the sportsman. Never the athlete. Only good at his work
and not allowed the clarity to focus only on it.

Jules was not above quoting him. Unattributed. Comments and jokes
and ideas Jules had taken from him. As though he were Jules' staffer.

Of course Jules did not tell him.

Got back to him eventually.

He was not anything but words in Jules' head to Jules and Jules took his
words to make Jules Jules.

It was not as though sinister doom hung above them or if it did it was
more like sunlight present and innocent-appearing than darkness.

Jules claimed a meal should be a ritual.

How could that be possible if one were eating a sandwich while
driving?

He did not believe in ritual.

Experience he believed could not be dramatized.

Jules said he was not going g anywhere.

Jules reminded him he would never own anything at a lake or in a
forest.

This before he was ignored.

Jules seemed nothing—a string of words. Penelope—Penelope.

Penelope's implication he was a psychotic.

The rumor Jules scrawled *freed of all that* on a wall. He did not believe
it. The fantastic quality of the allusion far beyond Jules' understanding.

The rumored Jules with his sportsman's affectations.

The bear they say will take the bait when baited for the hunt. In taking
the bait they say the bear will come and go as a ghost in the forest. If broth-

ers are not at war with each other and they hunt as they should in the snow of the deep woods.

Jules asserted Jules saw the absolute vacuity of everything. Why then the postures? Trying for a way out until Jules found the sole route?

The past would reach out and kill Jules. Hadn't Jules known that.

Had he, during the past?

Nothing in Jules but malice and all of Jules an elaborate and fantastic construct of Jules' malice.

Penelope adorned.

Penelope unadorned.

Jules a cypher.

Penelope a phantasm.

Jules existed only as a confused memory.

He would not exist.

Except perhaps as an inert memory of his former wife's.

Jules with the music creeping in.

How many times had he thought the same thing as though repetition were the essential element of consciousness.

His former wife after admitting her betrayal told him he should write Jules a letter detailing his disappointment with Jules.

Perhaps he should have written his wife a letter.

Or everyone else he knew.

Jules who could not throw away the thread from Jules' old hunting coat. As though if a thread disappeared so did Jules' shabby persona.

Confusion of desire, hope, happiness, despair, pain—he could not have described it. Being alive.

Jules deservedly gone.

Others gone undeservedly.

But gone.

All gone.

Teepee

He had to tell himself something. He felt if he did not tell something to himself, he could not get up and go on and do the things he needed to do, the basic things he had to do, like get in his car and drive to work. She had gone, and when she had gone, she said she would never speak to him again. That, however, was not strictly true, because a few days after she left, there was some problem with a credit card, and she had called him up to get him to straighten it out. She was civil then, albeit somewhat stiff. And for his part, when she had left, he told her he would never speak to her either, but he hoped she understood that he was merely responding to what she had said, which was, after all, a challenge, and so he could not have said, really, anything else. He had been pleasant and professional when she'd called, and he thought she might draw a conclusion—the correct conclusion—from that. He was willing to be friendly, friendly and more, but of course, he had to observe a certain formality until she was ready for that. But he, he had no doubt, was ready any time she was ready.

He told himself that she would call or email him at work. He realized he needed to believe she would, or at least could, call him to go on right now. She could call there, work, at any time of the day or night and leave a message on his voice mail. Suppose, for example, she had a message of deep, abiding, secret love which she was not, under the current circumstances, completely comfortable with telling him right now—at this moment, that was—she could leave it for him as a message, and then he could contact her and respond, sensitively respond, to her message.

This little idea, this thought, this belief of his wasn't so far fetched as to be beyond possibility or maybe even probability. He wouldn't tell anybody about it. He'd have this—his secret idea—and all the other ideas and half-formed images associated with it—all the assumptions, that cluster, that network of commingled ideas—he'd have all that, but it was only for him, it was for private, for his, consumption alone. *Network*—he never thought about that word when he used it. Like a net, a net cast wide, plus a work. A work being like a thing, or a construct. Was that like the German word *werk*? It almost had to be, didn't it? He would have to ask someone at the office about that; surely there was someone there who knew German and could answer a question as simple as that.

Meanwhile his secret thoughts could remain his secret delight. There seemed something delicious in this and something, related to that attraction, illicit. Was a secret thought a sin?

No, no, no. Couldn't he get away from all that? He had left all that as long and far behind as he could, as anyone could have left it, and here it was again. It was like his brother, the priest, that brother long dead to him beyond anything but the obligatory pleasantries, although actually that brother, so much older than he, still alive and healthy, *hale*, for maybe only the language of anachronism could accurately describe him, and one who would live, seemingly, forever, in the style of old priests.

Why this reflection before he had had his grape juice, and was there no end to it?

Then he was taken aback—back in time, for wasn't that where this damned speculation always led—and had he not, as a young man, often pulled on his boots and wished, frankly, he were a hero of the Old West? But this was not, he thought now, a literal wish. It was more of a broad aspiration. Not that looking in the mirror now, he could say it had amounted to anything. The discount stylist had done a terrible job; he had a ridiculous haircut, but there it was.

He cleaned up and drank the juice and ate a piece of dry toast and got in the car and drove to work just like he did on every other working day.

But his mind, to tell the truth, was not in it. What he was thinking of was the sticks in his back yard. Branches really—on Sunday, he had used his tree-trimming saw to trim the tree that was brushing his house. First he got the lower ones, the ones he could reach from the ground. Then he got up on a step ladder and got a couple of the bigger, higher ones even though it said right on the handle of the saw that you should never attempt to use the saw from a ladder. He had these special trash bags—robin's-egg blue—that were for compostable material. He had had to pay extra for them. He put the twigs and leaves in the bags, but he had three or four long, heavy branches left, and he wasn't sure what to do with them. He supposed he could cut them into short pieces, but he didn't have a chain saw, so he'd have to do it with a hand saw. What would come in handy was a wood chipper, but he was not going to buy a big, expensive piece of equipment for a few limbs.

Everything had been so much easier when they let you burn.

He thought, though, that he should strip those branches and use them as poles to make a teepee. There was a big, plastic tarp out in the garage that was just sitting there. He could arrange it on the poles and have a teepee easily big enough to sleep in. Oddly enough, the tarp was the same robin's-egg blue as the compostable-material bags. There was, of course, the question of why a grown man with a craft bungalow to himself would want to build a plastic teepee in his back yard and, by implication, camp out in it.

He got to work without incident, without hurry, and to some extent to his surprise, a little bit early. He had never been late. There was something about him that made him leave early so that he was always at least on time and almost always early. He got out of his car and walked, his head down as always, the head down, the shrunken shoulders, the sway-backed bad posture of it all—tired, he was tired already at 7:50, tired, really, before he had left his house, tired before he had gotten out of bed—and he was coming up to the main door when it hit him, the smell, that smell in the air, a complicated smell of the mixed smells of bacon and eggs and sweet rolls and ham and coffee and bagels, that motley of breakfast odors coming through the air.

There was a new cafeteria, and he had heard the food was better, but this seemed a little much. He looked up, and there on the top of the building was an imposing, shiny, steel square, a sharp chimney of silver sheet metal. It was a vent really. It must have come straight up from the cafeteria.

So now there was a food chimney.

He had already eaten; what of it?

Inside the metal light fixtures looked like ice-cube trays. He often noticed the tinny quality of the ceiling-mounted sprinklers. He couldn't remember, but he thought—he'd have to check his calendar—that today he was required to attend a meeting the consultants were conducting. That would take him, without doubt, to the meeting room with its maroon-fabric-upholstered-straight chairs.

Why this forever maroon upholstery?

These meetings—he went to several a week now, it seemed—were distinguished by the multimedia presentations, the bad haircuts, the oddly mismatched clothing. The last one, he had spent the entire time looking at his shoe, his shoe on his foot on his crossed leg. That shoe, he concluded, viewed sideways, approximated a triangle or a pyramid. After the meeting he had rushed to the men's room and then, while he was washing his hands, looked at the reflection of his head in the mirror. He had a ridiculous haircut, but there it was. So far, and so far as he could tell, he was holding his own. But not the guys on either side of his cubicle.

Was a sin a secret thought?

He contemplated opening his email, his voice mail, those repositories of possibility.

There was so much promise of something.

Once, at the German web porn site, he had to dream of a universal language.

He had to tell himself that the message might be there, but he could not stop from telling himself that no message would be there. The best, he heard himself telling himself, he was going to get was this pretty anticipation that could exist only as unknowing.

Why couldn't it be sweet sweet sweet—the way it was at first when they went to that Mexican restaurant and she was beautiful and he was—it seemed at least—charming and the food was delicious.

Later they went back, and the food wasn't so good.

He could ask her, when he returned her message, to go some place. He could try to make it sound like before, like the Mexican place.

These things that only he knew, these secrets, would die with him. He didn't have to worry about that. Of course, so would he.

I can not keep this secret from myself—that's what the poet said—the poet wrote that, in a poem. But why couldn't the poet keep a secret from himself?

All he wanted to do, really, if he thought about it, was to keep secrets from himself. He remembered later he had gone back and checked; he had the line wrong. That's not what the poet said. Not at all.

&
———

Big hunk of ice shelf broke off and fell in, some of it on TV, how big he did not know, big as a building or big as a city or big as half a small state, how would he know?

That ice important the TV said.

The ice necessary to our project.

Afraid that ice somehow—not now—some time—involved with him—not directly—involved with him in some bad way.

Maybe the TV said.

The rest, they had nothing to do with him, those people on TV, the rich, the celebrities, the politicians, the writers, the painters, the singers, the religious, the neighbors—any of them.

The Pop Star Of Good Intentions with his precious superior goodness should be muzzled or killed—told yes, yes, yes and put far out of sight—the ubiquity of virtue as identity, otherness. Was that all TV had for him?

Some preacher who could not shut up.

What with the Son of God and what was he—how was he—and with the Noble Savage—and he was supposed to compete with which when he could hardly see and was a poor athlete?

The story was—he thought—they were there in paradise, and paradise was not good enough for them, so they had to get out.

Or it was the other way. Paradise was not bad enough for them, so they wrecked it.

Something like that.

Had to be some fish under that ice or if not fish some squid or shrimp or creature. Something down there. And that shelf coming loose could be no good for whatever was below though maybe only a matter of displacement.

Displacement could be lethal.

He, after all, displaced from his once unhappy home.

Done now with seeing the future. Ice or no ice. He had not seen the ice—he had seen the TV image of the ice.

And *and*. She'd started every note that way but not with the word, with the symbol.

Ampersand.

And not a full ampersand at that.

Her ampersand like a plus.

Her ampersand like a cross.

That woman who was not for him.

He who was not for her.

The life that was not for them.

The world he could not abide.

All of it that ice and what did it or the dirt or the sky matter?

It mattered, he knew. It was that he could do nothing.

With her too.

He tried and she tried and they tried and ended.

End.

Circle

It was not as though he had no education.

Clearly he remembered once having watched an animated film. The film's main character was a circle. The circle circled around and sang:

> Your head's a bubble,
> Your head's a bubble,
> Your looking at trouble,
> Cause your head's a bubble.

There had been a point to him seeing this film, he recalled, but he did not remember what the point was.

Now the skin on his face was thick and coarse. Windburn, he believed, or age or drink and what difference did it make. Somebody said it could be a symptom of something.

It began to peel.

Turned out not to be a symptom. Turned out he had a syndrome. The syndrome that coarsened the skin of the face and caused it to peel.

Not the disease that coarsened the skin of the face and caused it to peel.

Perceptions of survival, he understood, were unique to no one. Every one, each one, had an individual concern.

His wife, Cassie, said, I told you it was nothing.

When he replied it was not nothing, it was a syndrome, Cassie said, that is nothing.

Maybe she was right. He hoped she was right. She seemed to know a good deal about these sorts of things.

Anyway a syndrome—a skin syndrome—how serious could it be? It was only a name for a condition he already had anyway, wasn't it?

He wanted to exorcise these devils of hope, of perfection, of a life other than quotidian and get to the business of contentedly hanging around inside his life.

He had no debt. The house, some hundreds thousands there, and the cars, thirty, maybe forty, but none beyond that. All right—no consumer debt. And most could not say that. When he'd bought the last vehicle the salesman had complimented him on that.

Yes, he'd felt good about that.

Sure, it took some effort.

Besides the film with the circle, he remembered a poem. From, was it, China?

> *The sky is porcelain,*
> *My heart is broken.*

Maybe not from China. That was all of it. Maybe western but in the Chinese style.

If he remembered, he'd ask Cassie.

She would know.

Kept track. That was part of it. Kept a notebook with him and tracked his expenses and obligations. An attempt to organize, to be organized.

If only he could get organized—really organized.

Where that anxiety came from.

Organized enough to function day to day. To see what his expenses and obligations were and meet and control them respectively.

That's where people got caught. Used the plastic and did not track what was going out. That's what the creditors counted on. Simple, really. Count on a little laziness. A little negligence. Get them where they were weak.

Keep them weak and in debt. A debtor society a consumer society simultaneously. A brilliance to it. Cunning bondage in the birthright for a mess of pottage sense.

People were fools. Bought the ads for the crap and the crap from the ads and the debt with the crap. If the credit structure were to collapse—well, near the end there was nothing but pander left. A fiction, obvious falsification of the world.

He could not imagine it otherwise.

Afraid. Afraid of everything we were not and of anything other than this.

When he had no idea, he looked, as anyone would, for a thing.

Cassie had wanted to see a movie. In the movie, a couple met early and constructed a love. Years later the couple met again and constructed a different love based on the myth of that earlier mythic love.

He did not know if Cassie were trying to tell him something but he was certain he should not ask her. He had told her earlier he understood that desire to learn a minor, an obscure, a fading language and to correspond only in it.

She told him he was being a fool.

He said he was serious.

She said he was mocking her.

He told her he had no idea what she was referring to, and he made sure he shut up after that. Day or two, it was all forgotten. At least, he presumed Cassie had forgotten. She was always reminding him of things he had forgotten.

Why not another language?

A language in which one might say:

> you can pick up piano, but you can not pick up a piano
>
> or
>
> you can pick up a saxophone but you can not pick up
> a ball game but you can play a pick up ball game or
> your radio can pick up a ball game.

Wouldn't this be better than that?

Than no payments till May of next year?

Than a man at the drive-thru who could not remember why he was there?

Dementia.

A man who could not understand himself as a suffering nuisance. Who kept learning and relearning the same things to what end. If the man were certain of anything wouldn't the man be certain he would never know?

It seemed dementia and credit were all one heard about any more.

He did not mention that to Cassie.

A woman with the presumed mother on one arm and the presumed daughter on the other outside the clinic. Kind of portrait almost.

Hadn't he in fact once studied biology under a professor named unremarkably, Grim?

The Biologist Grim.

He had a job he hated and a cyst in his mouth and a rage that sometimes made him feel he could pick up a car and toss it around.

But no debt.

None to speak of.

A stickered emblem of support on every car in his subdivision.

Except his?

Including his?

He was a man who stared straight ahead or he was a man for a man who stared straight ahead or he was a man for whom who he was for did not matter.

Everything would go as it went.

With or without him.

And the dollar falling.

Porcelain, the sky.

There was nothing to do.

Earlier—a week, a month, a year—earlier he had felt this way and told Cassie about it. Cassie suggested they go to a movie. At the time the suggestion seemed a suggestion so perfectly correct nothing could approximate it.

They went to a movie.

Later Cassie said, you cried at the movie.

Oh, he said.

Alphabet

I've wept tears of blood, he said.

Really?

She did not believe him.

Tears, anyway, he said. They felt like blood.

What about the alternate life? What about his alternate life? She did not seem to consider that.

His history.

He recalled how fifteen years before a man belittled him and berated his project. Did she consider that? He was not sure she knew about that. The man who had bitched at him was dead now.

Or that other one. That guy who'd betrayed him and tried to get his girlfriend at the time to drop him. She dropped him regardless; it was only a matter of time. That other one was dead too.

First that one, then this one.

One said this and the other said that.

They were not saying anything now. Indeed it appeared they could not.

Dead man A and dead man B.

Dead man A committed suicide.

Dead man B, he could not be sure. Maybe some self-infliction somewhere.

Only he knew what had happened with him and dead man A and dead man B. Only he remembered.

In a way it was a story. He could tell her the story if he wanted to. He had to ask himself if telling her the story would somehow advantage him. What good would telling the story do? And what if telling the story were to somehow disadvantage him.

It was quite a story what with God increasing the pressure on the narrative by killing off those around the protagonist.

That was maybe taking it too far.

You know, the arc and all.

Or was it a triangle?

He thought it was both—the two different models or something—the two examples.

Illustrations.

Dead man A and dead man B.

Both gave him trouble but he had not wished them dead.

Done him injury yet he was not delighted at their erasure.

After all, he was at least ambivalent about the erasure of his identity.

There was really no point in telling her the story.

Her name was Marie.

He might say, Marie, would you like to hear a story. He could end with and you know those guys who treated me so badly, they are both dead now.

It would be like he showed them.

He hadn't. He understood that. But in the story. The story would be like that and he might be well satisfied in giving her a story like that.

Marie might be satisfied too.

She was not cruel. That was not what he meant. He was just thinking that Marie might well be the type who finds a good story satisfying.

Dead man A was, in a sense, his teacher. Not in the formal sense. But dead man A taught him things.

That was why it hurt when dead man A turned on him. He was embarrassed. Dead man A told him his project was no good and he understood by extension he was no good.

He did not want to tell Marie all that.

That it still bothered him even though dead man A could not come back and repeat the charge.

If this story was working through to whatever end it was working toward, it was working beyond his understanding.

Dead man B had betrayed him, his friendship. Dead man B was his friend. That was why it hurt. Dead man B should have been embarrassed but he believed dead man B was not embarrassed.

Dead man B was proud. Proud of his betrayal of a friend because dead man B wanted to humiliate his friend.

He had been humiliated. He did not know why. Perhaps because he had trusted dead man B. Perhaps because dead man B had acted not as the dead man protested from desire for a woman, but out of pure malice.

Dead man B had hated him and he had not recognized it.

And so dead man B had been forced to demonstrate it to him.

Because he was a fool, dead man B had made a fool of him. In front of his girlfriend of the time.

It was raining.

Why the rain mattered.

At times it did not.

Why the rain sometimes mattered.

Who had said that?

He'd have to break the dead men apart if he were going to tell a story. As it was they seemed almost indistinguishable in death.

As though in death they had melded together.

And how would they like that.

Or what would Marie think?

For dead man A it had been a rebuke.

For dead man B it had been a gesture.

The gesture nothingness.

Raining.

He sometimes wondered what there was. Even now. After all this time.

The dead men had showed him.

Pathetic.

Pitiable.

Were pathetic and pitiable the same thing?

If a thing could not be distinguished from another thing, the two were the same thing.

He'd studied that.

Distinguished or differentiated?

So much forgotten.

So much to forget

The Hungarian Writer

—C'mon, he said, and do this for me. Like in the movie, he said, c'mon.
She would not do it.

He did not know if that meant she would not do it now or if that meant
she would never do it. Not never, he hoped.

She wanted to talk about a book she was reading.

He was not against books. For them, really. Or, in a sense.

The book was by a Hungarian writer.

He thought that a bit much.

What did he know about Hungary? He knew where it was. Maybe a
little of its history in and after World War II. That was it.

And this other thing.

She was talking about the writer's life.

And this other thing—

Account

—Hey, you're that guy, a guy said.

In the lobby. Some kind of hanger-out and where was security or was there no security? Besides, Bill did not know what the guy was talking about. He stepped back. Sometimes he felt like he was going up in an elevator.

The guy moved away from him.

All Bill wanted was to take care of his errand. Minimal human contact would suffice. Though that maybe was new; now that everything could be done without human contact, was the hunger for isolation greater than ever before?

The Japanese were rumored to have functioning sexbots. Why would it not cross Bill's mind?

The world being, what it was.

Pathogens being, what they were.

Not that Bill in any way shrunk from life. He was in the lobby while others—among them his acquaintances—performed their transactions via machine. So who was the live one now?

Who would be the live one later?

The sky, for example, in China. Bring that up in a minute on the screen and there you were looking at that—Chinese?—sky. Bill was not interested in denying the facts; why would he be?

The nonsense of the moment. The idiocy of the past. Well, time would lay it all to waste, would it not? And Bill. The end. The visceral fear, the cold paralysis in his bowel. The end. Bill could look forward to that. But he had to. Everyone did.

Or California. The sky there.

Sometimes he felt like he was floating on a raft. Or that he should get a picture for his wall. In the office. Get a picture and hang it up there. Others did. No policy disallowed it.

Was it *pisce pisce pisce?* That bird call like a foreign language. And *pisce.* Fish? Always some fish, Bill supposed.

He had noticed he was more sympathetic to men who shared his grandfather's surname than to people he met generally. This seemed as though it might be common to any number of people. Why should his experience be different than anyone else's?

When he was going up in the elevator, it felt like he was going up in an elevator.

Maybe the guy was trying to sell him something, the false recognition the basis of his pitch. Establish a relationship. Maybe the guy was trying to beg and Bill had scared him off. Transaction not completed. Where had the guy gone?

Man got all swallowed up.

Man got all disappeared.

More likely went around the corner. Find an easier mark. Maybe a victim of the cyclical debacle of the society's willing ignorance. Which one? Or both?

Bill had his paperwork in a manila folder. No one could fault him for that. Paperwork always made him uncomfortable though really he worked with paper. Always the fear some critical piece might be lost. Less an issue now with digital storage. But a pattern established strongly enough—

Too tired to contemplate the tiresome thought.

This was no California. For better or worse. Two sides to things. Half a life in these uncomfortable, necessary errands. Better than breaking sod with a spade in his Lordship's field.

Grip the loose sheaves tightly. Why? No complaint here. Nothing to wait in line to make his mandated election in a temperature-controlled environment.

Of course, a butcher's shop was temperature-controlled. He had the chance to get meat at close to wholesale. The problem was he could only get it in half-animal increments. Half a cow too much to store. Half a pig no small matter. Bill knew a guy. All quality. Straight from the specialty butcher. But it was too much. Buying half a pig, while not a solution, was strangely compelling to him. The put up and store mentality of the Midwest, he assumed. Funny how deeply those notions ran in the culture and how they outlived necessity.

He'd filled out the forms to move some money immediately and all for the movement of future monies into accounts that would, if everything went right, guarantee his future.

It was simple.

He had to make a mandatory election.

It was the right thing to do.

He was fortunate, though it would be a sacrifice, to have some money and the option to put it aside.

No China this. But sometimes he thought he was nowhere. He was not from nowhere. He was from somewhere, but it seemed like now he was nowhere. He came from somewhere to be here. To be here.

Though that was not his motive.

Half a pig—sometimes he felt he was nothing but appetite. Which had its purposes.

One had to admit.

He could make his mistake. Who better than he? Better he than someone else. He would have no one to blame but himself. He had no one to blame at all.

The magic of compound interest; that was what was supposed to work for him. He would sit in meetings, and while he did, his money was to work for him and guarantee his future.

His portfolio might become the notebook of his failure. He would lose it all. They would take it all. Might as well gamble it away. Might as well burn it.

This was what he was supposed to do, he reminded himself.

Other people did it.

Why did Bill feel the others could do it—were doing it—better than him?

Why did he feel as though he was compelled to await the workings of an un-understood formula which was not a formula at all, but, rather, a projection or speculation?

Out the window the sun in the sky, the cars on the street.

Those new cars all silver and angle. Wished he had a house like that.

A house like that would enable Bill to live in the future.

Those silvery cars objects, like spoons in a drawer. Bill had seen them pictured in magazines.

Yes no one *needed* him and yes he served *no function* or maybe *no identifiable function* or *no essential function* but why was all that on his evaluation?

Bill would not believe he was the only one.

Operating within his tiny realm of choices. The bigger outcomes predetermined. A transaction was a transaction. That was all. By submitting the forms, Bill was buying something. Why this buyer's anxiety? Why did Bill want to impress on the salesman that he was doing the right thing and have the salesman impress on him that he was doing the right thing?

The Chinese were about their transactions beneath their Chinese sky.

Outside the window like a movie.

The movies where the worries about the crises of the human spirit were still sometimes—albeit fitfully—expressed. The artificial future. The manufactured past. Football and cruise ships and the well-intentioned medium of the sometimes spirit.

You too can be a success. Seemed as though somebody was telling him that.

On television some kids in Africa or someplace wearing American castoffs. One in a donated fan jersey. That kid a world away in the jersey of a cause unknown.

What Bill had said was important, he was told, was now irrelevant.

What did Bill care; why this appetite for approval? Appetite. Yes. Appetite and its payment. Always the price. Penance the price of appetite. Why did that seem so emotionally true when it was empirically so patently false? Maybe it was, probably, it was, just him. There was a time when the past held Bill prisoner—he was obsessed with his failures in the past—all that held him for years. One day as he sat eating his combo meal in a fast food place with the other losers, some songs from his youth came over the sound system and refreshed him with the utter banality of the period. He reentered his youth, sojourned in the world of his youth, and recognized how bitterly he had hated it.

Today, however, this—all this—was about the future. Bill's desire for a happy future. A future he imagined somehow as outside the chain of love and habit. He knew better. Bill had been thoroughly indoctrinated in what to feel. He knew that and that there was no escape. If there were, he'd have taken it.

And he would have a different life, a life which would not have led to this or similar elections. The dream of another life the dream of another world really.

And there was no world but this.

One day he'd go see those masks at the museum.

He'd seen the ad on the bus. He'd taken the bus so he would not have to park.

A day in public.

—You could have mailed this in, the woman at the counter said. Or filed it electronically.

Bill said he knew. Pleasantly.

He knew.

Bill knew he would sit in meetings for twenty years more and end, like the dunce in a fairy tale, with nothing—with not even half a pig.

Fall

They—the he and the she of it—fell—and fell—and fell—and fell apart. He went his way. She went on with her life. These things happened as these things happened, and everyone understood.

He met a woman and fell in love. He and the woman married. The woman had three children from a previous marriage.

The man and his wife were happy.

The children were happy.

If there had been a dog, the dog would have been happy

Years went by. And years.

He quit smoking.

He quit drinking anything but red wine.

That, and water.

He ate less meat but still some.

One day he saw that earlier her.

She was in a parking lot. She was smoking a cigarette.

He went over and introduced himself. He thought of asking her for a cigarette, but he did not.

She told him she had three children.

She told him she was divorced.

He looked at her. He said, I want to ask you something, but I don't know what it is.

I've had three children and gotten a divorce, she said, for you. I've lived my entire life for you.

That's not it, he said.

The Descent of Value

He knew when he went in, when he got in, Selby wanted to talk to him, but he did not want to talk to Selby and never wanted to talk to Selby, yet he had to go in.

Had to remind himself of his age.

Other day, went through the drivethru, thought for a second of making the window girl, before he realized how far he was from all that.

Now Selby—Jesus Christ—what did Selby think—that anyone—any sane person—would listen to anything Selby had to say if Selby did not have the authority to compel the person—him—to listen to Selby.

Could not stop for a drink.

Wondered how much sick leave he had and how much eventually he'd need it.

I've been thinking, Selby said.

Selby held a book.

He knew the book—an entire book—could not be good. The memos bad enough. But a book.

The past, Selby said, is a broken system.

He would buy some liquor. That, and some pornography. Tonight on the way home.

But we can not, Selby said, disassemble or completely abandon it.

Always the fucking disassembly.

What did they do there all day in Arizona when they did not have to do anything.

Selby held out the book.

This, Selby said, is what we need.

He took the book. It was called *The Descent of Value*. He did not know what that meant.

I don't know what this means, he said.

Everyone, Selby said, is reading this. This is what will tell you what we need, where we're going. You have been in error, and this will help you correct things.

What error, he said.

This will make you see, Selby said.

Selby went away.

First the expert. Now *The Descent of Value*. The expert talked about what could and could not occur in a context. That was what the expert was an expert on. The expert talked about the law of contextual relations.

Or was it relationships?

Now that was over.

Experts fell like anyone else.

Like anyone might.

An expert an advisor in a way.

Like someone who might be on a council of advisors.

He was not on, nor ever had he been, any council of any kind.

He was supposed to have been something else. But he had not been.

He had never been anything else.

Something else beside the context.

The cycle of continuous innovation. That was it. All they were supposed to talk about was the context of innovation was it or the context for innovation.

He opened the book. Chapter called "Best Result." Another "Attitude and Producing Productive Change."

Was he supposed to read this thing now?

Would that satisfy Selby or at least placate Selby for the moment or the hour or the day.

Pornography and liquor.

Selby had arrived, as Selby often advertised, upon Selby's own merit.

"Making the Success Matrix."

This?

Get something from the past, from when he was young. Maybe feel young again. The players—roughly his age—scattered now, retired, dead.

Fortunate he had not chosen or drifted into such a desultory life.

He'd get that.

Could not bring it into the office. No longer could do this or that. The way it was now.

Told her once that life begins in mortal sin. Years ago.

In the lure of appetite he knew. Words in a pamphlet someone once gave him.

He'd get it though he knew it a game that held everything out—the holding out the game he knew—knew but knowing could not—that the twist—stop himself—he'd get the best, the ultimate, the final—the fulfillment of all that had ever been promised.

Flight

It was not him. It was some other man. In his house, a clock had been a precious thing. Almost every thing was a precious thing. His blanket. A thin, worn blanket worn nearly through when it came to him. Often he'd read, in those days, of prisoners with their thin blankets. And he identified with them, with his.

All imaginary of course. He was a boy safe and snug and not a prisoner at all. Yet he'd pull that thin blanket to his chin and pretend he was a prisoner. Unjustly imprisoned. He wondered why that fantasy, outside of the blanket, had had such appeal for him. A desire for a kind of order, perhaps. Perhaps any order no matter how harsh, so long as one could understand one's place in it.

He realized he did not want what he'd always said he'd wanted.

No, he wanted nothing of the sort, and thank God he'd never been close to getting it.

This realization about his spoken desires, much less some boyhood thought of prison.

It was too tiring to think about and he was too tired to think about it and thinking about it led to other ideas, other thoughts, other fantasies he had at one time or another entertained so tiresome that dealing with them would wear him, he feared, to nothing.

All of this as he sat cramped and strapped in an airplane. At least he was headed home. At least that. In spite of the weariness, the boredom, the discomfort and the thin- edged anxiety that even now accompanied him in flight, that.

And that before he thought of the poet.

He was hungry. He knew if he waited they'd bring him something to drink and something to eat—pretzels maybe or peanuts or perhaps a cookie. He was hungry because he didn't like to eat before he got on a plane because he didn't, really, know how his stomach might react, whether he might feel bad, feel worse than he always felt when he was on an airplane, so he was used to flying hungry. It was part of the whole thing.

The plane, the hotel, the plane.

The poet.

They had worked hard putting together what they'd needed to put together on this trip. Worked through lunch. There was no lunch. Stopped at a bar later, still working, and eaten some peanuts with the beer. Too late for lunch then. He had to work whether he was hungry or not. He owed his duty to work, not to appetite, although it was not this way for everyone. But he knew it was this way for him. It seemed at some time he may have had a choice though he could not remember making the choice nor could he identify the time when he might have elected to choose. But he believed he had—perhaps unwittingly—chosen, and when he had chosen, it seemed apparent now, he'd made the wrong choice.

So now if there was work—compelling work—he was compelled to work through mealtimes regardless of what the clock said.

It had something to do with loyalty. He wasn't sure how. Or to what.

And pick it up later. Get something on the way in or order something from room service at the hotel.

He'd never gotten used to eating in a hotel. Or sleeping in one. Those sheets. What if a virus lived in them? Probably not, mostly unlikely, but how could one know? And while a virus might not be there today, one could mutate and live there tomorrow. Didn't that happen every day? The viruses in the cooling tanks, in the dust, in the vegetable sprayers at the supermarket. The hotel dirty below the level of sight, fraught with microscopic menace. But he stayed there. More and more. More nights away every year. And for want? No use in thinking about that. Why let it torment him further? Why wouldn't it die?

He had asked himself, he was always asking himself, you want to spend the rest of your life in meetings?

It was the airplane. That wasn't all of it, obviously, but certainly there was nothing like the strapped and cramped experience of flight to depress him, to force some grim and pointless examination of his life he'd rather avoid. Why couldn't he relax, sit back, close his eyes, and dream himself free of this world, of this, the *this* of this, life.

It wouldn't be that long.

Below the brown fields looked like brown fields seen from above. What was wrong with that? Wasn't that enough?

A man breaks into a museum and breaks a clock. An eighteenth-century clock of gold and grace and mechanical precision. Gilt or gilded, something like that. Smash the thing to bits, but no more. Not to powder. Smashed it enough so the parts came apart and the insides—disconnected—were visible to all. Something to see.

A revelation, he supposed, in some sense of the word.

Of course the thing of beauty, the mechanical wonder, the work of art was destroyed. Things were destroyed every second. Why should a museum piece be different? Entire museums were destroyed.

Not by one man with a hammer, true. Not by a citizen of a putatively enlightened and democratic nation, presumably.

Though this citizen was. This citizen who had smashed the clock a continent away in a presumably enlightened and democratic nation. A nation, like many of the nations of that continent, with an interest bleeding into obsession with its language. It's precise language with a precise term for the smasher, a term translated as *the clockbreaker.*

Apparently they had enough of these clockbreakers to grant them their own noun.

It was hard to breathe in the airplane. The air was dry and stale and he felt a tightness in his chest and head. He hoped he was not coming down with something. The travel, the missed meals, and the hotels, more than anything the hotels, and now this mass confinement on the plane—it was a miracle he wasn't sick all a time. In every room, it was like he had to absorb the leavings of every guest before him, as though he were always in the presence of the ghosts of others with their germs their viruses their DNA left heedlessly behind in wait for him.

And he was leaving his heedlessly.

His samples.

The air in the plane worse though, looked at rationally. In the room there were one, two, maybe three at a time. Here hundreds breathed the same air. The stewardess had offered him a blanket, that thin, filthy piece of synthetic throw, used and reused. Not really a blanket all.

It was so beautiful. That was the comment ascribed to the clockbreaker upon his arrest. And either there was no elaboration in the press or the press was not interested in printing any elaboration there might have been. Made sense in a way. The press understood there was a point where you had to choke off the story. Left it neat. The deranged obsessive. The desire to possess or destroy. The beautiful sample so beautiful one cannot let it go.

All of that.

Or all of anything else that went into it. Still the clock was smashed.

Every sample, he supposed, destroyed and smashed in time.

Yes and the poet. The poet might have some understanding of this clockbreaker. It was odd, but he knew the poet. Odd because he did not often meet people like that—poets and so forth—in his line of work. And odder still, after he'd met the poet, that the poet had once off-handedly remarked that he had lost a brother.

As many people had.

He had seen the poet in a park on a breezy night when a group of poets was reading short pieces one after the next. Purely coincidental. He had been walking through the park unaware of the poetic event. But when he saw the poet, he went over and said hello and decided to wait and hear what the poet was reading. It was breezy and the poet was cold, so when it was time for the poet to read, he lent the poet his jacket.

Now crouched in this plane. Not much longer, and anyway, it was the all of it. Everything.

That poet dead now, he just heard lately, that poet, younger than he, dead some months.

And he looked out the window and felt what strange emotion as the plane was coming in low and thought how historically extraordinary, how rare in a historical experience, to descend as one witnessed his native city from above.

Verte

She wore a red dress that looked like it was made of silk, but he was sure the dress was not made of silk. The silky dress clung to her, and he noticed how she moved in it. Every movement seemed to him to hold a great significance, a heavy and beautiful sexual promise. He knew her, and he felt—really felt—that there was much he would learn from her and discover with her.

Yet he understood nothing. He was aware that he did not know how to proceed with her and that she would have to show him. He also knew that he did not know how to get her to show him.

When the time came, he would be in her hands. He did not yet think in these terms but he imagined, already, a future. The problem was he did not know how to get to that future. Though he knew he would get there through her.

He never presumed to ask how or why he believed she held the key to this future.

All he had to do was look at her in her red dress, watch her make the slightest movement, watch her smile at him as though there were a secret understanding between them, and then there would be no doubt.

He did not have a car.

She did, though, and they could use it. She could, and she'd take him along. And he'd go.

He couldn't tell her anything, yet they talked for hours. She told him about herself, and he told her what he hoped to do. He hoped to get away, to loose himself from the trap he thought his life to be. She believed he would. She listened to him and agreed with what he told her.

It seemed to him that no one had ever done that before.

She was open with him, open about her difficulties and her unhappiness, but she did not seem unhappy. She seemed to accept the conditions of her life with a quiet assurance that these conditions were minor hindrances to her inevitable progress. She possessed a self assurance that he admired and envied and knew he could never possess though he could not then have articulated this in those terms.

At her house they ate French bread with their meals; this was before French bread was widely available.

He never knew much about anything it seemed. What he knew about, the world he was in, seemed to be nothing to know, nothing to know about, that world was there all the time in front of him as though it were simultaneously the only possible world and a stone wall walling him in and any other world out.

He knew everything he was supposed to do, where to matriculate, what he was supposed to study, when to marry, what customs and ritual observances were required of him. He knew it all, saw it all in his peers, and rejected it all.

They were simple people. In a way, he was a simple person.

But in another way, he was not.

She came from a house where the kitchen chairs were like the chairs in a French painting.

Once he had gone to a classmate's house. At that house, they had to take their shoes off because of the expensive Oriental carpet. This was strange to him, so foreign; he could not understand the kind of life these people led.

She, and maybe she did not even know it, she was going to show him all that. She was going to guide him in those other worlds until he had attained an easy mastery of them.

She looked like the painting of the French woman, that painting from France.

This was what it was and the promise of everything too—all at once.

That was not to say that either one of them had any clear view of the future. He had no idea what she expected from him or why she was interested in him. He never thought about it, and if he started to think about it, he tried not to think about it. The same for the future. He had a notion of the future but no real idea. The future was all pleasant borders with a hole in the middle. That hole in the imagined future was inevitable. A complete imagining could only spoil everything.

Her arms around him as she whispered in his ear of the beautiful failure he would not hear. At the time he did not think about the God in his head. In a way, he did not know about the God in his head.

If he had been asked at the time, he would not have said that he was in pain.

His friends at this time were mostly acquaintances, the guys who spent the afternoon of the saint's day drinking and were, by early evening, puking up green beer. He felt he fit in well enough with them; they were pleasant enough, his fellows, but he saw no future with them. For them the military or the job site or the Catholic college and the business degree beckoned.

Not for him that future.

She, though, seemed to have two friends, two girls she had grown up with or knew through her family. Everyone he knew he knew through the neighborhood, but he knew dozens of people.

She seemed in her world to operate by different rules, but he could not understand whether it was a world of class or a world of femininity that dictated those rules.

The world had a texture. He could feel it in the objects. In the landscape. Some days the world seemed to bounce like a bright rubber ball. Other times he felt as though the leaden sky were upon him. There was weight to this world. Sometimes he was in a concrete cube that was growing smaller.

On her table there were crumbs. Bread crumbs. From French bread, those French bread crumbs on that French table that looked like another world.

There was no other world that he knew of but the future. The future, he thought, was a promise of a total engagement. He would be fully at work in work, fully in love at love.

Not that he would have the same table. He would, if he had thought about it, have acknowledged that he would in the future have some kind of table but he could not at that point have imagined what kind of table it might possibly be.

Wood maybe.

Or maybe steel and glass.

All this was against a backdrop.

When he was a kid, a little kid, he thought it was strange that there was always bread on his grandparents' table at meal time. Not French bread or anything—it was regular sliced American bread—stacked on a plate.

There was that and his familiar home life with his parents and siblings. That was another backdrop.

And his time at school and in the neighborhood and with his acquaintances, that was another.

There was another, too, mostly unrecognized, mostly so *there* as to be beyond the province of thought. It was hard and flat, that country, even where it was a little green, even where it was a little hilly. It was hot and cold and that sky was low and gray or blue and hazy. It was a place where life was small, and, if you thought about it, didn't mean much, no matter how big you thought you were in your skull.

That backdrop was there and you could be reminded of it if you needed to be, but usually that was not necessary.

And the smell. He sometimes forgot about that until he went out somewhere and was reminded of it. The green smelled green and had smelled green from the time he was a boy at the park. In the park there was a creek and the creek went over a waterfall and continued to the river. The banks were steep and heavily wooded and there were paths through the woods. He had gone to the park on a school picnic and the smell stayed with him, that wet, fresh smell of greenery with a hint of decay.

It was sometimes hard to remember, but that was a backdrop too.

That wasn't where they would be, though.

Their future would be in a city, but not, for God's sake, in this city.

It was a matter of saying the magic words, but to say the words, he would have to know the words first. At school, at his part-time job, there was no one to teach him those words. He looked to her, of course. Maybe they could uncover the words together. At school, at home, at work, everyone around him seemed to inhabit a vehement and crazed salvation. These salvations were individuated, though, as if each person created, maintained, and defended his own.

An acquaintance at work—they were dishwashers—told him in the stinking, steamy dishroom about the acquaintance's days as a commercial fisherman.

He did not know whether to believe the stories or not. This alleged fisherman seemed deranged, and he frequently drank on the job, but he was apparently a drifter who may well have worked almost anywhere.

This guy told of baiting a series of huge hooks, each joined to the other by heavy line closer to cable than the line of sports fishermen's understanding. This baiting had to be accomplished at industrial speed, and the hooks were played into the water as they were baited by some powerful mechanized winch or machine. If the baiter were hooked by mistake, he was pulled over the side to his certain drowning.

That would make, he thought, the fish fishers of men, down in their blue or green or black domain. There were all those fish stories where the fish talked, all the magic fish speaking their magic words. Down there in that water, dead on a hook, with the fish and other creatures to finish you. He knew better than to involve himself in anything much that might lead to something like that.

He would do *x* with the intent that *y* would result and little else.

She was waiting for him, but he did not know it. He suspected it, but he was not sure. He was possessed by an unyielding and nearly unconscious desire for certitude; he could not have said why. It was not that he was afraid to take a risk; it was, maybe, that he had so little that any risk seemed to risk nearly everything.

Not that he was poor. On a material level, he was comfortable. Not rich, but never hungry, either.

Fish kept coming up. Another acquaintance told him to eat fish, saying that it was pure protein. He could remember when it had been described as brain food. There was the theory, then, more or less from school, that humans evolved by eating other animals, that hunting or fishing up high protein catches allowed for the evolution of the larger, more complicated, human brain.

He called her up, but she was not there.

If he could have thought it, he would have thought, you be the vampire, Baby, and I'll be the king. If he could have thought it, he might have known what it meant. Something sexual and something timeless, but something more than that, he wanted her to transport him in time, so they could be timeless together, exist together outside time.

This only, of course, had he understood.

He did not know then that he might later dedicate himself to the study of, or the origin and development of the funeral card.

Instead, he was out in the dark with the TV for company, companionship, and dialogue. He had become Nixon. He had become Howard Hughes. It was America.

It seemed like he was always seeing ghosts in that screen.

Then he looked at the future, and he saw furniture.

Along with the furniture, and the paintings, and the green dreams of the future, his head was filled with the rule, the laws that governed his conduct and his thoughts. He did not know where all this came from, out of what book his actions had been codified.

He knew, in one way, that the law was just words in a book, and he knew he did not care about the law—those rules—that rule, but he wanted to be free of that book, and he knew, in another way, he would not be.

He smoked a cigarette in the rain and waited on his general relief.

He realized he was a cold fish. Only half-alive. He feared he'd find no deep feeling in himself. He hoped to someday live in a plastic house, and, by doing so, to be saved from terror, to surrender his fears.

He wanted to be done with it even as she was not there, but he could not be done with it. Was it—the rule, the fear, the lack—now, yes, a part of him?

He knew he had a future but he knew there was not any future for *him*. Whatever inhabited his head, whatever artifacts were accumulated there would not furnish him her, nor anything else he needed. He felt there something—he saw something in himself through her, something obscure swimming beneath the green surface of his consciousness, or not, and why wouldn't that be true?

Years later, walking up the concrete stairwell to his level, he noticed at his level what he had never noticed before: A huge green 3 painted on the gray stone wall. In the distance, someone was lecturing about the emergence of the earliest alphabet.

Later he asked himself if he remembered.

Remembered?

He had not realized he would have to do this. He had done *x* intending *y* would result, but *y* had not resulted at all.

If he could see it now, see all as it were, would it not be different, illusory, changed in every detail? Would not her dress have been green instead of red?

Faith

He and his wife at a social function. Public. Like church though he would never go to church. No church in him. No church for him.

Everyone knew that.

That other she there.

With her husband and children

The husband young with honey-colored hair. The children pretty and dark.

He tried to avoid her, but she came over. With her family. Whole family came over together as families are said to do.

Or are depicted as doing.

They were pleasant. He and his wife were pleasant.

Now he remembered she had always had that easy pleasantness.

She was a pleasant person.

He was not.

He a man made mean by circumstance and design and his own certainly errant sense of decency.

She had a complicated, expensive hairdo.

His wife remarked on it as he and his wife were leaving.

It's because she's French, he said. That's why.

Picayune

He smoked the kind of cigarette that killed you—the strongest one in the world. How could this document, apparently entitled "How to Make a Martial Arts Porno Movie," have come to him? It seemed more a polemic expressing the need for such a film than a guide to making it. On the cigarette box, unironically, there was a picture of a sailor. He would watch a movie like that. He would like to see a movie like that although he would never, ever, tell anyone that out loud. A shred of tobacco was lodged in his throat. This document a xerox of an email that someone had printed out, the text full of grammatical and spelling errors, a work defined by its desperate strangeness.

Yeah yeah yeah, the King, trapped in his regal popular culture and unable to think or dope his way out. Yeah.

Need—everything was about need. Somewhere. Somehow. At some level. He was afraid too. He was afraid he was burning himself up, himself and his needs. But the needs were burning too. The needs were making him burn.

Was that it, then, to burn yourself up?

Pleasure, okay. Pleasure had some funny definitions. Some funny incarnations. He coughed—this tobacco burned like acid. Pleasure and the flesh—pleasures of the flesh. Why not do everything? What was the difference? Study kung fu, smoke cigarettes, be the King. The live King, of course, with the dead King dead.

He threw the cigarette end in the street. With no filter, it would decompose.

He was too old, too soft, too lazy to study kung fu. Worse, he as a kid had believed in kung fu, but now he no longer believed. The movie, sure, he'd watch the movie. In the movie, there'd be beautiful, exotic women skilled in sexual techniques and kung fu. He was not sure if he anymore believed in sexual techniques. Still, they were something to see.

He thought as he went back towards the building that he could leave soon. Leave and go home and drink some whiskey. Try to forget his job and blot out his life.

He knew this was not the right way to think.

What about The Market? How was his attitude improving the performance of The Market? He was in The Market as everyone he knew was in The Market, and it was The Market that was the thing most likely to guarantee his future. There would not be a lot of use for kung fu or porno come Social Security time. There wouldn't be much use for Social Security either.

Didn't he realize that?

Like this six-page, small font, single-spaced email meant anything: What was the intent? Somebody wanted to make the movie, let him make the movie, and the movie's made, and there's the movie. It didn't even seem American. This seemed like something from somewhere else like France. Like some Frenchman made this orgy of violence and orgy of orgies and then presents it like it means everything in the world.

That's the way it was.

He had to live with that. And with himself. Though he knew how burdensome he was. But this other apparently had no idea what a burden each one was to all those around him. And everybody else as bad, the loved ones as bad to us as we to them.

He couldn't stay in this doorway. He had to go back inside.

Everyone had to be somewhere, even this computer-crazed Frenchman, and he had to be here for a while yet.

Get his orgy on film. Send out his message. That'd put him on top. He'd have something then. That was the other, that was the other one's life.

He couldn't get that. Go back in, go back out, drink some whiskey. He knew it. He was settled. He was settled with his problems intact. But he had to go back in and appear, at least, to be making an effort. Always, always, always there was some going back. Even if there was nothing, if he had nothing to go back to, he was sure he would go back *mentally*. *Mentally*—that was the only true time travel.

With that he got the headache.

A quick headache, a pain at the front of his skull that lasted maybe a minute, maybe less.

Someone, he thought, had shot a beam into his skull.

Funny how he thought that. He did not believe that. It was just something floating around, something from the TV.

Regardless, he had to go back in for some more time.

Couldn't it just pass? Couldn't he just sit in there as though he were in a trance? Why not be in a trance? He saw himself as a man with a desire to be in a trance state. If he had that movie, and he put it in his VCR and watched it, he could sit there as though in a trance. He could watch it again and again.

But he might not be in a real, an authentic, trance. Why, he thought, was he denied a trance state? It wasn't part of his culture, true, but how long did he have to suffer at the unknowing, the uncaring, mercy of his culture?

What did he get? Instead of the trance states he got, what, the Promised Land? The problem with the Promised Land was that inescapable and unenforceable promise. Instead he got to go back inside and toil by the sweat of his brow. Or something like that.

Okay. Yeah, all right. He had this temp thing writing curriculum for inclusion in a software package. Right, right, right. He knew how to do it. He, he, he had been a teacher.

He should have brought some whiskey with him. You know, in a little flask. But that would be bad. He couldn't let himself do that. Just as he couldn't make or participate in the making of a martial arts porno movie. Wasn't in him. Wasn't who he was. Or could be. Prisoner of his culture, his idea, his ego, his head. Couldn't think his was out. Couldn't *feel* his way out.

Somebody's, not his, escaping the ego. There was a trap to be sprung. Nope. Not his.

Back to the Spook House, one way or the other. Earn his daily bread.

He knew a woman. Yeah, yup. She was brilliant then. Now she sold things or helped sell things. He had been a teacher. That was supposed to be better. Really he had helped people so they could be well prepared to buy things. To consume things like the movie. To take the movie, the stuff, the food, the cars—all—into themselves, in a way.

He took all that into himself. How could he not?

The best thing would be to live in a box.

But then—

The best thing would be to live in a box with her. He could be King then and reign with the Queen. Reign in this Kingdom of Junk.

Museum Piece

They were to take the pledge first.

The despair pledge, he believed. Not that the pledge embodied or contained despair, but the desperation around the constant marketing of the pledge. More noise as though there were not enough noise to make one despair.

Then, at the museum, the display of the work of the celebrity photographer and on TV the special about the same celebrity photographer and in the paper the review of the same celebrity photographer's books of photographs. Apparently something was going on or nothing was going on and someone was trying to make something go on or he and everyone else was supposed to think something was going on.

He was tired of it.

Exhausted.

Somebody had taken a picture of him at the company holiday party. In the picture, he looked awful. He looked exhausted. He looked at the picture, and he could not believe he looked as bad as he looked in the picture.

Perhaps he did not.

Whoever took it was no photographer and the camera was cheap and there was no composition and the angle was so low and crooked and strange one could not intentionally duplicate that angle.

A picture, so what? He was not a movie star. A bad picture did not mean anything.

He had not asked anyone to take his picture.

Nor, really, had he given his permission to be photographed.

It was a party. He had to go. He had, to the extent he could, removed as much social pressure as he was able from his life. The holiday party—he had to go—and have a drink—only one—hold a bottle of beer for two hours—

sip it—until he had been there long enough and could leave and go home and have a real drink.

He did not know if the people at work hated him. He thought mostly they did not think about him as he did not hate them and he did not think about them.

He had no authority.

A picture was what—light and paper and chemicals—then—now less—some arrangement of electrons—really almost nothing.

Epistemology

He did not feel good.

He had not felt good.

He knew he would die.

Not now.

Not because of how he felt.

He would die later when the time came.

He knew each of us would die.

It seemed unfair those he loved would or had.

Not so much for him.

There were others.

He could have said something to the others.

He should have.

Not now.

They were dead to him.

They were not dead at all.

The one of course he had loved her.

We can not be happy. She said that.

Then there was life. His job. Or career. And what he did. A frenzy of acquisition, it seemed. That sustained him and left him nothing.

After the movie, he warned her no two would couple as such, knowing they already had.

She did not know what he meant.

He did not know what he meant.

Met her years later at a mall that was and was not a marketplace.

You wanted, she said, a perfect love—the love of God.

All he'd been through.

Did you expect, she said, the perfection of Jesus Christ?

From me, she said.

He did not know what she meant.

Balance

TV showed success, the programs, the commercials his rebuke. His failure which needed no reminder.

He could quit watching. Or go straight to video.

Success there as well. With the occasional failure. Or something in between.

Nature maybe. Only nature videos. Or videos that depicted the natural. What was natural. What came, more or less, naturally.

What was failure but an imbalance in power?

Like this guy at work. This guy at work manically solicitous and entirely false yet apparently genuinely craving affection and approval. Though this guy would turn for the slightest advantage, real or perceived. He'd take your affection and approval and betray you immediately and delight in his betrayal because his betrayal was your failure and his success, and he believed your failure and his success were abundantly deserved.

Everybody at work was like this guy.

It was the way work worked. Indeed, he suspected work might not work at all if it was not for this.

Tried not to have any part of it.

He was not doing very well.

He had never done very well.

In a way, he did not care. In a way, he did not feel it made any difference, for he did not believe in his work or in his coworkers or the purpose of the enterprise whatever the purpose of the enterprise was.

Could get along with what he had.

And less.

Was he to move towards—to—austerity?

Skill?

Accomplishment?

All that over. All that none of it for him.

At work he was already accused.

Accused though no doubt his motives were transparent.

Then again perhaps his motives were not.

Maybe his work was. Or his attitude towards his work. His attitude. That was it. Wasn't someone always saying he had a bad attitude? Wasn't everyone always saying that?

Sometimes he wondered if anything but pain and death were true.

And what happened.

Whatever that truly was.

As when he'd attempted the clumsy reconciliation of love.

No more of that.

There would be no rebirth. Not for him. He was glad of it. He did not say that. But it was true.

Part of the TV the promise of endless variety and not just the TV, the broadband, the music, the magazines, the media, the culture—all that mediated universe.

If everything so varied, why this sameness?

Gray future projected out the gray past, the cycle cycling more quickly, more ridiculously, to no objection in the gray moment.

The suburb of his despair.

The world of just this.

Not that he had to—

He could embrace it all.

At work a person pretending to be excited asked him if he was not excited. And expected a perky response.

He suspected—he did not say—suspected the mask of excitement a component of a planned humiliation.

A test.

He failed. He knew.

One

All varieties though all variations of the one. He could not stand it. They walked streets dressed—each gaudy costume calling—a demand or invitation or a demand for invitation.

And they talked.

Earpieces wired and wireless as they went connected to whomever they spoke to about whatever they spoke about.

Costumes, yes, for him, for anyone who looked, but the words, while not private—public was public—the words for someone else, someone specific.

He was not worse than everyone.

He was not better than everyone.

Simply he was unattached.

Alone.

They apparently not though that was not certain for though he was alone, he talked to people all the time, but he was not a man for an earpiece nor public displays of communication.

Often he had little to do.

Because of circumstances.

Few people had the same—identical—circumstances insofar as they did not find themselves where he found himself in these sorts of circumstances.

They had other concerns.

Because he had fallen out.

Because he had given up.

He had fallen out and given up because he could not keep up; he could not keep up because he could not understand; he could not understand because he had failed to stay with it, to be current, to get it, to be on top of it, to get inside of it.

That was the end.

He was told he was done.

He understood what he was told.

Not like Bergstrom. Bergstrom was perfectly in tune with the popular culture and thereby understood every reference and allusion and could communicate in terms comprehensible to everyone he met with everyone he met. And communication was essential for if one could not communicate with someone how would one ever get someone to offer up his or her money for the important services Bergstrom, and formerly he, was in the business of selling.

The answer apparent.

Even to him.

And if to him, certainly to everyone, to all the people who knew—who effortlessly understood—more than he ever had and more than he ever would.

There was no dispute.

He—belonged—where he was doing what he was.

He had thought of killing Bergstrom, but he immediately understood another would take Bergstrom's place, that there was—in the sense of permanence—of finality—really no killing Bergstrom.

Not that he would have.

Not under the circumstances.

Not while knowing he had no culture, popular or otherwise.

And feared—

Feared without—

Without what he knew he did not and would not have.

Feared he had or was nothing at all.

All that nothing.

Yet he walked the streets.

And watched. Watched them as they talked happily in bright costume and costumed in the element—weather.

Fine day.

Could not be a finer day than the fine day that was today.

Bergstrom had a calendar that said something like that. Won it as a prize or an award. Result of Bergstrom's perfect knowledge or perfect feel or perfect pitch allowing Bergstrom to be perfectly in tune.

Tough once he'd been right. Or he'd been good. Or he'd been adequate. Something.

He'd been that.

Fine weather.

Yet.

He felt something.

The agitation of spring. As though there were some possibility of something. That sense of possibility entirely false yet so strong so strongly felt as if it had always inhered in him though it had not.

The disaffecting world.

The world disaffected.

His loss of position no end of appetite.

He'd pick one and follow. Listen. Hope to hear the intimate things—something of hers intimate, and find excuse to talk to her, one of them wrapped brightly like fancy holiday candies in a store window, she'd talk and he'd talk—and she would then—and then—he wanted then—then—he wanted.

Furniture

Ankle went, worse this time. Urgent care doctor—a cheerful Pakistani—
said, this does not look good. Ordered a splint and care at minimum after
he'd refused crutches and the ominous, black-velcroed boot.

Looked bad. Shin bone straight, foot twisted entirely away. Could not
move it back.

He did not want to go back to therapy.

Therapy.

Ice. He iced. And splinted. Rested heavily on his cane. All as ordered as
though this the beginning, the harbinger of a long cure.

Worst the immobility. Elevated the swollen foot and sat in a chair.

Sat there.

Listened to the radio.

Watched TV.

Saw the antique show. People brought things in. Some valuable, some
junk. Lady with a chair. Chair by a famous maker. The appraiser said the
chair was beautiful and unique and exquisite and gorgeous and fantastic.

The chair looked OK to him. Nice. Pleasant design.

The lady happy the chair was worth so much.

Who'd blame her; he wanted money too.

Antiques.

Normally he would not watch.

But the swollen ankle.

Knew the word for it, term for it from the Greek, what good did that do
him? Or his ankle?

Maybe made it worse.

Maybe not.

Stupid thought in enforced idleness.

Could idleness be enforced? If it were, was it truly idleness?

145

Useless.

Put the famous horse down. Nothing to do with him.

Still, he to sit there and listen to it.

Or grab the cane and get up.

Happy at least with the cane. Got it at the drugstore. Chrome. 19.99. Adjustable. And worked, he presumed, as well as any cane. As well as a cane, say, double the price.

Riddle of course he knew.

White foot on the white towel over the ice pack as a fish on ice in some market. Cold. White. Dead.

Spontaneous injury.

No one said that. Was not, as far as he knew, a term. Merely a description.

Maybe not. Nothing spontaneous about it for all he knew. Some structural flaw devolved to structural failure. Years maybe in the making. So where was the spontaneity in that?

Sudden. Yes.

Sudden not necessarily spontaneous.

Glaciers melting on TV.

Immobilize the ankle and put ice on it. Not real ice. Blue chemical ice pack the doctor'd given him.

All that melting didn't some of it always occur. Not glaciers. The snow. Didn't snow in the Alps melt and the Romans collected it in aqueducts and piped it—maybe piped it in the aqueducts but collected it in reservoirs—he had hadn't he seen an aqueduct once in France, outside Arles, maybe.

Could not remember.

Desultorily, he paged through the desultory local newspaper.

Nothing he could do about glaciers.

Whatever was going to be over had already begun to be done.

All fine and good to sit there and feel destroyed though this was not destruction yet.

In that paper a picture of the economic prophet. Economic prophet coming to town to give a talk about the economy—talk that like the prophet's book had made the prophet rich. The prophet had gotten rich by telling people who weren't rich the rich people were right and if the people who were not rich wanted to stay ahead they had better be educated and creative and flexible and innovative and try to get rich or else.

Some old story he'd read thirty years ago, the story fifty or three hundrd or two thousand years old then.

Empty.

A husk.

Still, back again, again.

Wished there was a movie on TV.

A gangster movie.

From when—they used to—they used to give you then, the chair.

Hook

He told people the rifle story because he enjoyed seeing how people reacted.

Or had told it.

He had not told it for years.

At one time, he had kept dogs. House dogs, not outdoor dogs. Dogs that lived in his house and waited for him to come home.

Near the holidays, he had the dogs photographed in Christmas hats and Christmas sweaters.

If anyone said anything bad about the food, he could not eat it.

If anyone said anything questionable about the food, he could not eat it.

He was with what was right then and now was wrong or with what was wrong then and now was right. Now he was with what was right now and would later be wrong or with what was wrong now and would later be right.

The idea of putting forward that story long past when the story's done as though the story were still alive when it was not.

And make my beaker a pitcher, he'd read, that I might tumble down.

Even the archaic language of drink sounding now like prayer.

Definition like a broken cookie on a glass coffee table.

Now I am going to get drunk, he said.

Reply

He'd heard that the flowers replied; he knew about the sad geraniums, and he was not thinking of them, nor the tree of light, nor that scene in the porn film that had so impressed him as a young man. None of those storied images seemed important or even relevant to his situation.

He'd hurt his leg; that's what he thought. Some knee, hip, ankle injury he could feel in his aching bone. He could not remember any traumatic event; he considered arthritis or some need for replacement joints. It was difficult to be certain, but it seemed his back was involved. No surgery. Not for him.

He had the leg injury and in time it was chronic. Maybe because he'd done nothing about it. Perhaps it would get progressively worse. That was his recent thinking.

And he woke up.

One morning that was, and when he woke up, although he remembered nothing strenuous in the night and his chronically-aching right leg ached chronically, his left leg ached sharply. He got out of bed and twitched and lumbered, each step uncertain, painful, and realized he was walking like someone he'd seen, someone twice his middle age.

When he got to the bathroom and looked in the mirror, he saw tears of pain in his own eyes.

This, he thought, is very bad.

Then he inhaled deeply.

It seemed what he must, in that moment, do.

The next moment problematic.

Gingerly lowering himself to the toilet, he shrieked.

Certainly he was concerned about the future, about repeating this experience daily.

It was nothing.

He told himself that. People, hell, people lost limbs, mobility, everything, and he had what? Some pain in the legs? Pain, that for all he knew, might be easily cured if he would visit a physician.

If—

And even if it were incurable, if it were, say, a tumor on his spine, some ugly lethal package, it was still nothing.

That was what he needed to keep in mind.

He hobbled downstairs and, not knowing exactly what to do, turned on the television. Somebody was on there singing something. Then the singer talked. He did not get the singer's song nor did he comprehend the singer's references.

His vision of himself was slipping; maybe that's what it was. It was more and more difficult for him to understand himself as the knowledge that every day millions cycled in and millions cycled out was increasingly apparent to him. It happened.

Like nothing.

Failing legs might be the start. Insofar as there was an identifiable start. Really, the selection of an arbitrary event in a series, he supposed.

He'd tripped and fallen down a half-flight of stairs a week or so ago. Nothing serious. Trip, crash, scrape. That was all. But he noticed he was anxious now. Tripping over his own feet.

Twice today he'd nearly fallen.

And he knew what that meant: It meant he was aware how frequently he nearly failed and he was counting now. The count would be daily now.

It was nothing.

If he fell again he'd fall again, all this consciousness nothing but worry. He no longer believed in himself.

That was it.

No longer believed in his life. That he had an individual life.

Why should he?

Used to be fate.

Used to be written.

It was all written. Now, not written. Videoed, one supposed. Of course. The film. Or now, the digitalized images of one's life. That was how one imagined the narrative of one's life now.

What could be simpler?

The outraged commentator in the next room delivering the commentary of outrage.

He'd been, lately, wearing his special shoes. He did not tell anyone, but he was happy with the shoes and the fact they were, after all, special. The idea was the shoes would help heal his legs. But not, obviously, enough. In their effect. Not in the idea.

He'd heard the woman singing so beautifully and thought it's all—all this—in the song.

Pleasant thought at the time. Not enough forever but maybe all that was necessary for that moment.

The wet, partially-rotted smell of the world.

So much of his life, it seemed, in a trance, a reverie. That and an investigation. Every little dissection. Every little parsing of each tiny thing an argument with itself and every other thing—an argument against the world.

Well, he had not done it right.

Find your life in a pop song, that was it. A flimsy picket, perhaps, for belief and any sense of solidarity, but probably no worse than most in human history.

He sat and looked out the sliding door at the dark.

Here he was.

Earlier he'd believed he would be elsewhere.

Hard to say.

Here he was thinking of the reply. It wasn't—was it—one must suffer oneself incessantly.

Sword

Somebody gave him a samurai sword. Not a real samurai sword, a replica. But with a real blade sharp. It was a gift. Something somebody thought he would like.

He liked it.

He would have liked to mount it on the wall above his desk.

He could not.

The company had a zero tolerance policy. No violence in the work place. No weapons on the work site. Of any kind. Not even pepper spray.

And he did not have a desk. He had a work space. No, that was not right. He did not have an office; he had a work space. He did not have a desk; he had a work station.

He did not know why these differences mattered, but the company was very clear about these things.

So the sword was at home. In a closet.

He did not know kendo. Or escrima. Or fencing.

Sometimes he wished he knew these things. Or some things like these things. But he did not.

Furthermore, he was not going to learn them.

A person like him did not have enough passion for these things to commit to them. He knew without doubt the commitment was substantial.

If someone wanted to be any good.

He lacked the passion.

The energy.

The will.

Why should he do anything?

He did his job and paid his bills and taxes and honored his minimal family obligations, and that was enough.

That was all.

Maybe in the past—

He had no love for the past.

Some sentiment, perhaps.

Driving in, he'd seen workers digging at the side of the road. They worked in the rain. Long time since he had worked outside in the rain.

Some day he would be dead, and he would do nothing at all.

His work neighbor had pictures of her kids on the walls of her work space. That on one side. Guy on the other side had pictures of Jesus.

Tried not to talk to that guy.

If that guy could have pictures of Christ, why couldn't he have a sword?

Maybe not call it a sword.

Maybe call it a work of art. An heirloom. Was there a policy against heirlooms?

Thought about ratting out the Jesus Guy, saying the Jesus pictures offended him, but that would make the Jesus Guy believe the Jesus Guy was being persecuted because the Jesus Guy believed in Jesus.

Woman with the kids perfectly nice. Probably a good mom too.

If the Jesus pictures came down maybe the kids would have to come down too.

He could not remember the rule. Maybe it was a law. The directive came from legal.

He'd had a wife.

His wife was gone.

She'd said she was leaving and he'd said, If this is because of my drinking, I'll quit drinking.

He was trying to buy some time.

It was not because of that, she said.

It was because of what he was not, she said.

He was not tempted to put up her picture.

It seemed pathetic.

A memorial to their unhappiness.

An empty frame better.

There was a time he'd hoped for everything and tried to get it and all that led here.

Here.

Now.

He suspected he had perhaps learned something.

Not that he regretted anything.

Not anymore.

2.

The memo said the company was sputtering out fast. Been through this before. Sometimes the company failed. Sometimes the company was reenergized.

He was not energized.

Afraid of more failure.

Certain amount of failure inevitable, but too much, corrosive.

Lethal.

That totality always at the bottom of things.

More bedrock than lurking.

Maybe the Jesus Guy could pray for the company.

Pray for this occupation.

Or sink into the acceptance of the world as sinking into a grave.

His grave.

Or abandon himself and somehow continue to exist.

Impossible. True terror of life—finite, inseparable, indistillate.

Company could go on without him.

Leave him merely unemployed, unpensioned, ruined. At an age he'd never get a comparable salary.

Unable to retire.

His wife had said he thought he lived in a story and he should try living in life.

He told her she was insane.

Comment did not help.

He could start looking.

Spent half his life looking.

Enforced insecurity ceaselessly revisited. Not only him. Everyone now as the jobs went and the infrastructure broke and the politics failed and the TV—the TV—got even worse.

Everything he knew on the way down and something he did not know on the way up.

Him too. Some man he was not coming forward.

He did not like it.

He could not stop it.

If she were saying anything, she would say she had seen it all coming.

If she said that, he would not believe her.

It was all—not recognizable, not foreseeable, not predictable—all of it was luck.

Not luck, exactly.

Fortune.

He could not say that. No one believed in fortune. No one knew what fortune was.

To assert fortune would be like advocating the divine right of kings. As a man with a sword might.

But not him.

Maybe not fortune. Maybe something more diffuse, a loss of focus.

The end of focus.

Maybe he could ask her for some cash. At his humiliation. Take the humiliation for the money if she had any and might give it out.

He'd sell the sword if it were worth anything, but it was not.

Someone had given him a book.

About swords.

The weapon that cuts and stabs, it said.

She'd look coy if she gave him money.

She was very good at looking coy.

Better than him. He'd grant that. Even without the money. For free.

And why hang up a worthless sword but to have—to assert—some identity. At work.

Did he need that?

Did he want that?

And what the payoff in that?

3.

He would wind down.

Fall back.

Retrench.

Lower his standard of living some more.

Not as if he could not.

Did not need much.

One day, he knew, he would not need anything.

Some satisfaction in that.

By default, perhaps.

Not that he was immune to commercialized pleasure. Conditioned as everyone else. Who could or would resist? Why?

Why would one?

True, his lowered standard enforced upon him. Were it otherwise—

He'd be the same as anyone, right?

And that was right, wasn't it?

A lower standard would not kill him.

It was the again of it all.

That everything repeated a little weaker, a little worse as he became less, a little less with every reiteration.

Inevitable lessening repetition as though some image repeated and faded from itself.

When he stopped thinking he was something other than this, he stopped thinking he was anything at all.

While he was not a theorist—there was no department or office of theory in the organization—he had the most theoretical work. He cited, for example, casually, for example, The Law of Enclosed Populations. In a context of course.

That would go with the rest of it.

His own fault. What was he doing?

He sat at his computer and searched swordswoman and got the bad fantasy art, the half-softcore goddesses as genre and Japanese cartoons. This at work when this was not his work.

Sword.

Christ made some mention as he recalled. Or two.

Or that story of the couple in bed with the sword between them and what story was that or fairy tale?

Separation and division. As he'd read he thought not in a book but on a matchbook all those years ago when he'd smoked twenty cigarettes a day, the spiritual figure depicted not with the sword of violence but the sword that severed truth from illusion.

Like her from him.

Or truth from fiction.

Or wealth from poverty.

Dark from light.

This from that.

Picture Show

1) Notebook

Used bookstore he picked up a paperbound copy of Camus' notebooks. Volume 3. No. He could not. Not all that. Years ago, yes, yes, all that. Then. Now. Now? No. Not now.

He read the 1st sentence. Knew. He bought it. He'd read it. Brought it on himself—years of doing nothing but bringing it on himself or more likely bringing himself to it.

Looked at himself in the shop window why not. Slack puffy face, swollen body like some hulking movie monster. Him. The him he'd made himself. And why?

Knew he could not bear to explain it to himself again. He had his reasons. He knew he had his reasons.

Hadn't everyone?

Reasons explained nothing. Held nothing. Supported nothing.

Now back to that, hulking there, the stained and shopworn Camus in hand.

2) Mallet

He'd taken the goddamned Yugoslavian rifle apart knowing he should not, and he could not get the fucking Yugoslavian rifle back together having known he would not. Sweat in his eyes. Hands covered with cosmoline and blood and solvent.

Cut himself of course in the course of his efforts, and why not, that certainly as known, as easily predictable, as anything else.

The entire assembly hinged on the trigger assembly which literally hinged on part of the magazine but which, properly placed, seemed impossible to seat.

Yes he had instructions.

Yes he was trying to follow the instructions. Held everything in place with his left hand.

Mallet on the workbench.

Rubber.

Smacked the trigger guard twice. Pretty good blows but measured.

Seated right in.

The mallet concentrated the force.

3) 1970 something

In the boy town. It wasn't called that. The store had some weird name, the name a tortured reference now as obscure as it was stupid. He thought of it as the boy store. Bad part of town. Front room all marijuana pipes, butterfly knives, vaguely biker paraphernalia.

Back room all hard core pornography.

Did anyone say hard core anymore?

Did core mean anything any more?

Wondered would he run into anyone he knew. Unlikely. Anyway what was anyone he knew doing there any more than what he was doing there?

Looking for a movie. He'd seen it almost 30 years before in a theater when there were porn movie theaters.

Wanted to see it again.

Remembered bits and pieces. Maybe remembered wrong.

He wanted to know.

Was pornography still pornographic after 30 years? Was it, instead, now quaint? By comparison?

Maybe he'd buy a butterfly knife too.

Confused the pornography of the '70s with his life.

4) Theater

Someone gave him the tickets. At work. He could not say no. He had to go. Seemed like any number from his department had to go. He feared he would be required to demonstrate his gratitude and enthusiasm. Enthusiasm or maybe it was excitement the new requirement.

The new loyalty test.

So he went.

Parking was awful. The weather sleet. Enough to put the roads in question.

Why did he never anymore wish to leave his house?

Every seat taken. Like being on an airplane. His place the middle of the row.

Two-hour monologue. One actor. No real set. Maybe some tricks with the lighting. He could not be sure. Monologue seemed to be about self-awareness and despair.

Two hours.

Acting. All this acting out stories for God's sake.

Though there was no story here.

For God's sake.

No story.

Monologue.

When did the monologue take over and why did it replace whatever it had replaced.

5) Couch

Up when he had to be up. When his body awoke itself. Wanted to sleep, but he could not get back to sleep although he was exhausted, exhausted from drink, he got up.

Nominal coffee and sitting in a chair for awhile, sitting. Ate something later which was good or which was bad.

Lay on the couch.

Read the book. The book of the day. Book all in one day. One book. Or several. Another book the last day of the protagonist's life. Still one day but different, almost a different genre of book.

He fell asleep.

Napped as though dying. Not quite as though dead. As if he were being drained but was not yet entirely drained.

6) Weather

Sunday and Spring more or less and more or less 2 choices: poison or shooting. Get the poison at the garden supply. Hook it up to the garden hose, thread the bottle on, spray the mixture of poison and water on the lawn.

There were instructions.

For the poison to work, it had to be sprayed at least 2 hours before the rain.

The bottle warned about this.

Breezy and cool.

Or shoot.

The ranges were open to the public and he'd vowed this year he'd practice and this year when hunting season came he'd go.

Something other than the office, the couch, the books.

Had that rifle together.

Breeze seemed to blow the clouds in.

He did not know if it just seemed that way.

Rain.

Too windy to poison, too wet to shoot.

7) Forgiveness

Thought of things he would never forgive—slights, insults, humiliations. Some women. One certainly. Maybe none. Would have to think were there more than one but if one had to think about whether someone had done something then did it not follow that the person had not done something unforgivable?

The unforgivable immediate. Immediately recognizable. Not subject to forced recollection.

He knew that.

8) The Woman

Dead to him now, dead as their relationship, and he no doubt dead to her, dead and forgotten.

Zero.

Nullity of it all.

Of everything dead.

Though he had heard—where had he heard—some reference to the whispering dead, the dry whispers of the dead barely audible, incomprehensible, hardly in the range of hearing.

Heard as the dry leaves moving in the wind are heard.

Always at it, the dead.

9) Suicide
One he knew well. Other he knew to say hello to, not truly a suicide, accidental, self-inflicted gunshot while hunting, knew him pretty well. Another one he knew well.

Neighbor, attempted, gun shot wound, knew her slightly.

Another attempted, wrists, knew well.

Barely knew one shot herself in the head.

Maybe there were more.

He could puzzle them all out, but he did not want to puzzle them all out.

None for many years. None since he was an adolescent.

The one murdered.

Years ago too. Around the same time as all the rest of it.

10) Dream
He'd dreamt he'd gone to see the madwoman. Many years earlier, the dream took place. When he was in his twenties. When he'd go see the madwoman. In his dream, the madwoman was in town so he went round to see her.

At her parents' house.

She stayed there when she was in town then.

He talked to the madwoman and the madwoman talked to him. The madwoman became agitated and he became angry. Then she was angry.

A door slamming. That in the dream. In real life, he was not sure.

Her parents' dream house exactly as her parents' real house.

Except the location wrong.

In his dream, the streets, the grid of the streets of this, his native city, were reversed. North/South ran East/West and vice versa.

11) Work
So he had his job. Where he worked. His office. In the bureaucracy. Somebody asked him what he did—he had given his meaningless title—and he tried to explain it. To summarize it.

He'd tried to make it sound like a job a grown man would have.

A job with some pretension to being a job worth having.

He'd talked about the budget and tracking the categories and managing the projections and the fact that, while he was trying to do all that, the people in the field were constantly calling or emailing because the people in the field were always running into problems they could not solve or questions they could not answer or, more frequently, were simply seeking reassurance that their answers, advice, and solutions were the correct ones.

Done, he could see the questioner had lost interest.

12) The Uncle

The Uncle old for decades, sick for years. The cousins sent money and received money and did the legal things but the cousins had left the city early and were leading profitable lives of success elsewhere.

The Aunt long dead.

He looked in once in awhile. His Uncle. The associations with the past.

Inescapable family.

Any kind of family.

Once a brilliant man, the Uncle, a professor or something like that.

Why these things so forever unclear?

The Uncle reduced in his age and illness to mere cunning. Survival. Greedy. Out, as why would the Uncle be otherwise, only for himself.

The Uncle had a number of doctors. Mostly old like the Uncle. All reliable prescribers.

Who knew how many doses the sleeping pills, pain pills, tranquilizers, he stockpiled?

Every morning the Uncle got up, dressed carefully in suit or coat and tie, put on his shined shoes.

Suits out of date and white shirts yellowed, yet suits all the same. Shoes worn out yet shined.

Dressed, coffeed, lightly-breakfasted, the Uncle took his pills and sat on the couch.

Periodically, he'd take more.

Dressing every day to stay home and get high.

13) Trip

His Uncle needed some documents. The documents in a neighboring state. The agency would release the documents to him if he had a signed release from the Uncle, but he had to go in person.

In person?

Now?

They would only give the paper over to a person.

What bureaucratic demand for efficiency that a human must appear to be dehumanized?

A cruel elegance to it maybe.

Wait until technology ensures such a visit unnecessary, then require the visit.

He had to go. He would not take the Uncle. Four and a half hours each way for ten minutes in line at a window.

Drove over and got the paper. Turned around. Stopped for lunch at a chain on the beltway. The chain styled as a family-friendly place with a regional, an "American," theme. A simplified reflection for self-congratulation with false comfort food and reasonable prices.

Had to respect the marketing.

And the food, what was promised. Okay.

Stood in a pool of piss at the urinal.

Back on the road. Half an hour out from town, he stopped at a bar with a Western theme. Exurbia. Maybe the place had been there for years. Quiet enough, a few workmen, a few locals.

Drinking beer when the bikers came in. Middle-aged, riding the big bikes from their suburban homes. No outlaws. Hobbyists. Living some statement or fantasy or icon of freedom away from work, the house, the kids.

People his age.

People like him.

14) She

She'd accused him of delivering a harangue—a deranged monologue unending.

He'd paused.

15) Media

The radio played a rap song about another rap song.

Column in the paper about another column.

He turned on the TV. Golf and programs about remodeling houses.

He lived in a house.

His house not unlike the ones being remodeled.

See his own life. Like everybody else. Everybody seeing his own life repeatedly. That was right wasn't it?

Watching.

16) He wrote

I asked her for her silken flag, a studied imperfection raise'd like a pink pencil.

He wrote.

17) Quality

Quality day at his job. One every year. Speakers brought in. PowerPoints. Exercises. Teams.

Teams, for Christ's sake.

And this year, this year, they brought in the Billionaire.

Why would the Billionaire come to Quality Day? Not for a speaker's fee. Somebody knew him or was related to him or maybe he had to serve some community service. Even billionaires that, sometimes.

The Billionaire talked about quality.

The Billionaire took a few questions.

He stood up. They could not very easily fire him. He asked the Billionaire about the team and the stadium and the taxes and the schools.

The hard question.

The Billionaire was gracious, his answer intelligent and detailed.

He realized absolutely media and sports and government were all the same.

He thought of the heroically dead athlete.

The government did not need to force the media or even to tell the media.

The media knew how to make the story and how to tell the story and the team got its role and it was all like something fifty, sixty years ago.

18) Another woman

Gone to the acquaintance's house for the acquaintance's anniversary celebration. Barbecue. He did not know why the acquaintances had invited
him. Fill out the crowd, maybe, to make the party more special for the
acquaintance's wife.

The acquaintance introduced him to a woman. Pleasant enough. Younger
than him. Attractive. It occurred to him he was invited to meet this woman;
immediately, he realized that could not have been the reason.

They talked. The job. The neighborhood. Some movie.

The woman was devoted to a popular musician but fiercely opposed to
another popular musician.

He did not know much about these musicians, but it seemed to him
their music was similar. When he mentioned this, the woman became
excited and explained in animated detail how the two had nothing in common and why her favorite was vastly superior to the other.

He apologized and told her he had not known what he was talking about.
She walked away.

19) Later

He told the Uncle about the woman. The Uncle appeared to be pretty high.

You thought it was something else but it was only this, the Uncle said.

He did not reply.

The Madwoman had said, perhaps, something the same to him once.

He had not replied.

20) Supervision

His Supervisor called him in.

That had not happened in a long time.

Ever get burned? His Supervisor said.

Ever get cut? His Supervisor said.

He did not understand.

Ever burn somebody? his Supervisor said.

Ever cut somebody? his Supervisor said.

You know what I mean, his Supervisor said.

21) The Uncle

In paradise, the Uncle mumbled, we will make our peace in some way we
need not now understand.

What, he said.

What, the Uncle said.

What was that, he said.

I was asleep, the Uncle said.

22) Hallway

Noticed a pattern, cocoa-colored on the off-white tile. Some drip, drip,
drop as though a juggled cup of burning coffee spilled with the carrier's
steps. Liquid dried now to clot as though paint in some abstraction.

23) Comment

He remarked to his coworker, Stevenson, on the oddly static quality of
middle-class, middle-aged life.

Stevenson looked at him blankly.

Forget it, he said.

They'd been assigned to work together.

24) Project

The project was a survey. He did not know how to construct a survey, how
to avoid making the questions biased, the results unreliable.

But it was a satisfaction survey. Satisfaction with the department.
Internal and external stakeholders.

Who cared what they thought?

Design, actualize, distribute, collect, collate, analyze.

Design meaning write.

Actualize meaning finish.

The rest, the rest.

In addition to his normal work.

Everybody pulling together to get through this.

This the ongoing manufactured crisis.

It was a living. Stevenson said that.

He did not disagree.

Unclear what the results—useful or meaningless—were intended to be used for.

Perhaps to support the existence of the department.

Or to answer some mandate. For quality.

25) Dialogue

The quality people were putting on a show, and he was told to attend. His Supervisor said his attendance was mandated.

Mandated?

Nothing had ever been mandated before. Some things were clearly requested but no emphasis on the fact they were required.

He had to register. The department paid the fee, but he had to fill out the form. He got the brochure. Glossier than he would have predicted. More professional.

How much money was there in quality?

The show was in a hotel in a suburb. He'd have to cross the city at rush hour to get there.

The brochure said quality concepts would be explained in a series of dialogues.

Two women did the dialogues. One had been on a TV commercial and the other had a background in community theater.

These two women—actresses—would speak out—perform—the dialogues.

And he was to learn about quality by watching.

26) Motel

Crazy man lit a fire at a motel. The crazy man believed his wife was in the motel with some other guy. A couple people got killed; most got out all right.

The firemen put out the fire.

The policemen captured the crazy man.

He saw this on the news.

The crazy man ranting into the camera as he pulled against the cuffs and the restraining officers.

Unclear whether the crazy man's wife was in the motel or whether the crazy man had a wife.

Ex-wife, more likely.

A relative said the crazy man had gone off his medication.

27) Psychology

Perhaps the Madwoman was not purely responsible for the pain she had caused him.

Perhaps she had things—emotional things—she could not resolve.

He, after all, had things—emotional things—he could not resolve.

These useless, irresolvable feelings.

But what was that?

Psychology?

He was sitting in his car in a parking lot. He had left the office to get lunch. Leaving the office to get lunch was, under certain conditions, permitted.

These conditions were not absolutely clear to him.

No one had ever explained them.

Or someone had and he had not paid any attention.

He had got a hamburger at the drive-through and pulled over in the parking lot of this decaying strip mall. Trash blew around in the wind. People went into the dollar store and the discount liquor store and the failing video store.

He ate with the doors locked and the engine idling.

The radio was on.

A popular song playing.

The music pleasant, comforting.

Soothing.

The purpose of popular music.

28) Error

Stevenson asked him if he had tracked and submitted some reports. Those reports should have gone two quarters ago. Stevenson said somebody from auditing had called.

Auditing, he said, they're always a couple years behind.

You sent them, Stevenson said.

Of course, he said, I remember doing it.

He could remember doing it. He did it on a cold day. It was snowing. He watched the snow fall outside his window as he waited for the reports to print.

He remembered.

With all the precision of error he remembered and was certain he could not be wrong.

He had not sent them.

He might suggest, he might imply, he might all but state he had sent them and they were somehow not properly received.

29) Circle

He had gone to the quality dialogue before the error. After the error he received a memo from his Supervisor, inviting him to join an in-house quality circle.

He did not know if it was because of the error.

He knew he had to accept the invitation.

The circle comprised of people from various departments. It met Thursday afternoons after work. On site. No chance of a bar someplace, casual drink while they suffered.

No.

Worse than that.

Mandatory reading list. Schedule. Assignments. Presentations. Like a fucking class for Christ's sake.

No additional compensation.

All this at the direction of someone he'd never heard of with a title he'd never heard of: Director of Continuous Improvement.

Improvement?

Continuous.

In his department which was responsible for doing the same things again and again in cylindrical calendar?

30) Daze

He thought he was dazed. That he lived in a daze. A dream, a jingle, a riddle, a joke—some worn out consciousness of radio, print, TV—of sad songs and stupid ads and premanufactured emotion.

Overwhelmed at times by the sheer stupidity of life, his head full of nonsense.

And what else?

And what better?

The endless spiral of appetite?

31) Collapse

The Uncle collapsed in a drugstore while the Uncle was waiting to get a prescription filled.

The call almost routine. The hospital worker explained clearly and calmly the Uncle was out of danger but tests were being run and the Uncle was being monitored.

He told his Supervisor he had to go to the hospital.

The Supervisor did not respond.

He told about the collapse.

Go, the Supervisor said.

Drove as quickly as the law allowed.

Parked.

Got to the desk.

And through to the curtained section of the emergency room.

He thought he might be doing this a number of times.

The aid drew back the curtain for him.

The Uncle monitored on a gurney. A priest beside the Uncle. The priest quietly reciting the Hail Mary.

Never thought of the Uncle in any religious context.

The priest called Father Robert though the name first or last unclear. From Saint Barbara's.

The madwoman's name was Barbara.

The world of no connection.

The priest one of the new new priests.

The Uncle who made a living of failing continuing.

32) The Madwoman

Her name was Barbara.

What had he wanted from her.

Someone had told him to make a list. A list? Some emotionally-healing method from a magazine or talk show.

He'd do without remedy.

She had written him: *What was between us seems like madness.* Struck him like something from a book, but everything seemed like something from a book.

Maybe, she wrote, *we could meet again and talk.*

Talk, he wondered, what talk for what with what imagined or imaginary result.

33) At Work

At work his Supervisor said, Hey, you remember Fuckhead?

No, he said.

The Supervisor handed him a memo and said, Well, remember this, Fuckhead.

34) Afterward

The Uncle, they said, was fine. Which meant the collapse had left him no worse than he was before he collapsed. The Uncle persuaded somebody to give him another prescription.

The collapse more, apparently, an interruption than a collapse. Caused by blood pressure or blood sugar or inner ear or who knew what.

Causation vanished.

Cause it seemed did not matter.

The Uncle said he'd been attending St. Barbara's for years.

Could that have been true?

35) Magazine

Saw a magazine at the gas station. 208 sex acts inside, the magazine said.

The specificity of pornography.

He could buy the magazine.

A forbidden transaction.

Forbidden by whom? If he did not stop himself what could or would stop him?

Habit the forbidden.

Habit the arbiter.

36) Holiday
He read the American middle class burned a forest in its fireplaces at the
holiday.
    Read the triangle as the foundation—precursor—of the pyramid.
    Of civilization.

37) Movie
Stevenson asked him if he'd seen the movie.
    He'd never heard of the movie.
    His Supervisor had seen it.
    Stevenson said the movie was a noir version of the video game. The
effects, Stevenson said, were fantastic.
    What do you say to that, his Supervisor said.
    He did not have anything to say.
    I'll have to check it out, he said.

38) Circle
At the quality circle, he was given a T-shirt with a logo and slogan on it.
The quality circle facilitator led the group in chanting the slogan.
    He had thought that was a Japanese thing.
    Or maybe calisthenics were the Japanese thing and the slogans were
Korean. Or Japanese. Or simply an Asian workplace thing.
    But he thought all that had long gone by.
    Rejected as inappropriate for America, how had it managed to come
back? Who decided these things?
    The culture, he supposed.
    The culture of the workplace or management or something.
    He did not know.

39) TV
After the circle, he went home, opened a tall boy, turned on the TV.
    There was a movie.
    The movie with everything.

Everyone in the movie troubled because everyone in the movie caught between two worlds.

Everyone caught between everything and what solace to be found there he understood.

The music cued his understanding.

Solace.

Of course theses characters only existed during the movie.

40) Collapse

The Uncle collapsing regularly now. Every six weeks or so.

The doctors could not find one thing, any specific cause.

He did not know what they meant.

Maybe the Uncle was simply weak.

More likely all those pills. Or some in bad combination with others.

The Uncle would not stop taking them; he was certain of that.

The Uncle would continue to collapse.

41) Beard

Stevenson came in on as Monday with a full beard. Stevenson had been clean-shaven on Friday.

The beard looked funny.

Three days?

He could not ask.

No one mentioned it.

42) Dead

None of the suicides had hanged themselves. Most, the vast majority, used guns. And there was some cutting. No gas, he thought, but maybe he could not remember, some car exhaust in one attempt.

Hanged man a deeply rooted image.

What with the Tarot.

And Christ, of course.

One image maybe derived from the other.

Movies, the popular executions of the past.

Hanged man a common sight once.

43) Barbara

He wondered would it be like that man in the story who goes to the depths of the forest and finds nothing there.

That she might be nothing.

Nothing to her.

But perhaps a picture.

Maybe some words in his head.

What did he want from her?

44) Conversation

He had to talk to her.

He could not talk to her.

He knew he had to talk to her, and he knew he could not talk to her.

He knew.

He had a dream.

What if his dream whispered to him she had done everything and he had not known it.

He knew she had not.

Nothing whispered to him.

Nor spoke.

Nor shouted.

45) Book

Everyone in his quality circle got a book. Not the same book. The leader decided who got what. Everyone had to read his or her book and report on the book to the circle.

His book by a former psychiatrist about the psychiatrist's journey from believing in psychiatry to a spirituality to an understanding to the application of that understanding to organizational dynamics to create a methodology to revolutionize institutional culture.

He showed the book to his Supervisor.

His Supervisor flipped through the book and threw it at him.

We got no budget increase, his Supervisor said, so instead we'll have the revolution.

Lead the way, Fuckhead! his Supervisor said.

46) He wrote
He wrote: The abandonment of the word and the aspiration to a pure calligraphy.

47) Doubt
He had his doubts. About the Uncle. About the job. About the Supervisor.

He suspected everything about the Supervisor, from the tight black suits to the razor-sharp click knife the Supervisor carried, costume in some theater of ego need.

The TV now said blueberries were the healthiest thing to eat.

She'd said she wanted to talk to him.

The quality circle said it was improving something.

48) Talk
If he could talk to her, he would try to make her cry.

If he could talk to her, he would not try to make her cry.

If he could talk to her, he would not.

49) Confidence
He told Stevenson he thought the quality circle was idiotic. The compulsory role playing and feigned enthusiasms, he said, were produced by morons for morons. All of this, he said, had to be obvious to the department's management.

Stevenson did not say anything.

That was it, he said, to hone his disgust to indifference, his indifference to silence, his silence to nothing.

Now, he said, he understood.

50) She said
This is my whole life, she'd said.

What happened between us, she said, seems like some kind of madness.

51) Department Meetings
Each meeting now featured a PowerPoint. No questions were taken. All documents were emblazoned with the quality motto. The motto framed in every workspace. Everybody required to fill out a brief self-evaluation form at the beginning of every meeting.

No one knew what happened to the forms.

The activation memo was referenced.

Nobody knew what the activation memo was.

52) The Supervisor
The Supervisor called him in.

You have a mother, the Supervisor said.

Yes, he said.

Ever sing you a lullaby, the Supervisor said.

I'm—I don't, he said.

Of course she did, the Supervisor said. Doesn't matter what it was. Doesn't matter if you remember. The words don't matter.

No, he said.

No. They're sounds. Pleasant sounds to make somebody feel better. Make the sounds, listen to the sounds, and feel better. Understand?

I guess so, he said.

Make sure you do.

53) The Uncle
Kept collapsing.

Still no diagnoses.

Father Robert had given the Uncle last rites at least seven times.

Then the Uncle collapsed and died.

He was at work when it happened. Worse he was not at work but on a work excursion. The excursion organized by the Quality Director. Something between a school field trip and a convict's journey.

After the tour of the state of the art facility, they ate a preselected meal with nominal dessert at the same family chain he'd visited during his trip to the neighboring state.

The final collapse, as best he could discover, about that time. About the time of dessert.

54) Money
Left quite a bit of money the Uncle, none of it to him, though he was named to arrange the funeral.

Indifferent to this as he understood his long-understood obligation.

He understood obligation.

The rest he'd thrown all away, but this he could not free himself from. The Uncle an uncle, regardless.

55) Dialogue
The Supervisor emailed him they had to meet for a dialogue.

The Supervisor also used dialogue as verb.

Each fad its jargon, this jargon the ghost of the fad.

This dialogue might be the end for him.

56) Maybe
Maybe do something. He thought that could be it. Get out. Get away. Maybe go hunting in the snow as he had always wanted to.

Then remembered he had once hunted in the snow and had not got a goddamned thing.

57) Show
During the dialogue, the Supervisor used the archaic phrase *picture show*.

Picture show?

58) Instead
Maybe he could not talk to Barbara but he could write her a letter though he hated to have anything written between them—too fixed, too permanent, too unalterable. Maybe send her a cassette.

Cassette?

A CD?

Whatever it was now.

Record it instead of talking.

59) Count
The Uncle moved now to the column of the dead.
Counted with them now.
No love for the past. Though perhaps some sentiment for it.

60) Surprise
He was not fired.
Stevenson was.
For taking pills at work. He'd thought they all did that—that they were all medicated but him.

61) Arrangements
Making the arrangements he felt he had been through all this before, and if he had done it before why must he do it again though he knew from TV the past kept happening again and again.
He called the cousins.
He did not attempt to imagine their lives.
He did not characterize the Uncle as an ambiguously willing participant in the Uncle's decline.
Barbara—he would have to call her—all the rest, all accumulated.

62) Invitation
After the Uncle's obituary appeared, he was invited to join a worship circle.
The worship circle based on the quality circle.
Join our family, the invitation said.

63) He remembered
Are you going to tell me to fix things with Barbara? he asked the Uncle.
Who's Barbara? the Uncle said.

64) New memo
He'd been going to the circle and keeping his quality journal as the quality leader required quality circle members to do when the new memo arrived.
Looked like quality was on its way out.

Are you ready to Commit to Total Team Commitment, the new memo said.

His purchasing power declining with every new program.

65) What

What would he say to Barbara other than the fact? After that, say what? Sing her the quality song? It had been a chart reduced to a rhyme—a chant—now a song.

66) Caution

Hey Fuckhead, the Supervisor said, the President is giving an address.

The radio on his desk was playing. He switched it off. He was not sure if it was the President of the company or the President of the nation.

Stevenson said he was Stevenson's *only friend* in the company.

Now Stevenson sent an email describing his *arrogance* and *bitterness* and *presumption* and *hatefulness*.

The Supervisor said something about rollout.

67) Funeral

He paid for the funeral and for the funeral dinner in the church basement afterwards.

The cousins would or would not reimburse him.

Barbara was not there.

Maybe she had not gotten the message.

Maybe she had other plans—a trip—something she could not reschedule.

Maybe she could not do it.

At the dinner, he sat across the long table from Father Robert.

This skein of obligation the way it was and could be no other way being who they were, he understood.

The priest looked at him.

He looked at the priest.

He went home.

Nothing.

Carbine

Maybe he had a sore that would not go away.

He had a sore that would not go away.

Anything could get in there. Remember that.

He could seal it up, but not all the time. If it were always sealed, it would never go away.

And open, anything could get in. If everything was potentially everywhere in the bacterial, in the viral, sense, everyone knew that these things traveled, if not how they traveled, then anything.

He felt a deep desire bordering on compulsion to buy a carbine. Oh he'd kicked the idea around before. Idly. Now it was different.

In a sense, he did not need a carbine. In a different sense, he could imagine any number of scenarios in which a carbine would be immensely handy.

He had the money. He happened to know he could get a perfectly reliable, perfectly durable carbine for under three hundred dollars.

He had three hundred dollars in an envelope in a drawer.

He mentioned it to some of the fellows at work.

They asked him why.

I don't know, he said.

He didn't know.

He could sit in his apartment with his carbine. In America, there was nothing wrong with that.

To cradle the carbine would be to heft the perfection of balance.

The answer to the questions implied by our collective collapse seemed buy a carbine.

And if it were right in America, how could it be wrong anywhere?

He knew many were wrong elsewhere. Many, many of them. It was on television and anyone could see it.

He knew he might buy a carbine and hold it every day for a few weeks or months and then put it aside and what then?

Then what?

Some of them at work told him this carbine would lead him only to trouble.

Trouble.

In a world where he might vanish or be paralyzed or end lying helpless in his own filth?

The Juniper Prize

This volume is the fifth recipient of the Juniper Prize for Fiction, established in 2004 by the University of Massachusetts Press in collaboration with the UMass Amherst MFA Program for Poets and Writers, to be presented annually for an outstanding work of literary fiction. Like its sister award, the Juniper Prize for Poetry established in 1976, the prize is named in honor of Robert Francis (1901–1987), who lived for many years at Fort Juniper, Amherst, Massachusetts.

LaVergne, TN USA
14 May 2010
182714LV00001B/43/P